Marx
Abbott Hardy Machiavelli Chesterton Cooper Emerson Joyce Austen
Defoe Melville Montaigne Haggard Hugo Grimm
Eliot
Stoker Carroll Christie Molière
Wilde Maupassant Byron Schiller
Garnett Fitzgerald Engels Smith Kafka Hall
Goethe Einstein Hawthorne Willis
Cotton Dostoyevsky
Baum Kipling Doyle
Henry Nietzsche
Leslie Dumas Flaubert Turgenev Balzac
Stockton Vatsyayana Crane
Burroughs Verne
Curtis Tocqueville Gogol Vinci
Homer Widger Tolstoy Whitman Busch
Darwin Thoreau Twain
Potter Freud Zola Lawrence Plato Scott Harte
Kant Jowett Stevenson Dickens
Andersen Burton Hesse
London Descartes Cervantes
Poe Aristotle Wells Voltaire Cooke
Hale James Hastings Irving
Bunner Shakespeare
Richter Dante Chekhov Chambers Alcott
Doré Swift da Shaw Wodehouse Benedict
Pushkin Newton

 tredition®

tredition was established in 2006 by Sandra Latusseck and Soenke Schulz. Based in Hamburg, Germany, tredition offers publishing solutions to authors and publishing houses, combined with world-wide distribution of printed and digital book content. tredition is uniquely positioned to enable authors and publishing houses to create books on their own terms and without conventional manu-facturing risks.

For more information please visit: www.tredition.com

TREDITION CLASSICS

This book is part of the TREDITION CLASSICS series. The creators of this series are united by passion for literature and driven by the intention of making all public domain books available in printed format again - worldwide. Most TREDITION CLASSICS titles have been out of print and off the bookstore shelves for decades. At tredition we believe that a great book never goes out of style and that its value is eternal. Several mostly non-profit literature projects provide content to tredition. To support their good work, tredition donates a portion of the proceeds from each sold copy. As a reader of a TREDITION CLASSICS book, you support our mission to save many of the amazing works of world literature from oblivion. See all available books at www.tredition.com.

Project Gutenberg

The content for this book has been graciously provided by Project Gutenberg. Project Gutenberg is a non-profit organization founded by Michael Hart in 1971 at the University of Illinois. The mission of Project Gutenberg is simple: To encourage the creation and distribution of eBooks. Project Gutenberg is the first and largest collection of public domain eBooks.

My First Visit to New England (from Literary Friends and Acquaintance)

William Dean Howells

Imprint

This book is part of TREDITION CLASSICS

Author: William Dean Howells
Cover design: Buchgut, Berlin – Germany

Publisher: tredition GmbH, Hamburg - Germany
ISBN: 978-3-8424-5208-4

www.tredition.com
www.tredition.de

LITERARY FRIENDS AND ACQUAINTANCES

by William Dean Howells

CONTENTS:

LITERARY FRIENDS AND ACQUAINTANCES—First Visit to
New England
BIBLIOGRAPHICAL

Long before I began the papers which make up this volume, I had
meant to write of literary history in New England as I had known it
in the lives of its great exemplars during the twenty-five years I
lived near them. In fact, I had meant to do this from the time I came
among them; but I let the days in which I almost constantly saw
them go by without record save such as I carried in a memory reten-
tive, indeed, beyond the common, but not so full as I could have
wished when I began to invoke it for my work. Still, upon insistent
appeal, it responded in sufficient abundance; and, though I now
wish I could have remembered more instances, I think my impressions were accurate enough. I am sure of having tried honestly to
impart them in the ten years or more when I was desultorily endeavoring to share them with the reader.

The papers were written pretty much in the order they have here,
beginning with My First Visit to New England, which dates from
the earliest eighteen-nineties, if I may trust my recollection of reading it from the manuscript to the editor of Harper's Magazine,
where we lay under the willows of Magnolia one pleasant summer
morning in the first years of that decade. It was printed no great
while after in that periodical; but I was so long in finishing the
study of Lowell that it had been anticipated in Harper's by other
reminiscences of him, and it was therefore first printed in Scribner's
Magazine. It was the paper with which I took the most pains, and
when it was completed I still felt it so incomplete that I referred it to
his closest and my best friend, the late Charles Eliot Norton, for his
criticism. He thought it wanting in unity; it was a group of studies
instead of one study, he said; I must do something to draw the different sketches together in a single effect of portraiture; and this I
did my best to do.

It was the latest written of the three articles which give the volume substance, and it represents mare finally and fully than the others my sense of the literary importance of the men whose like we shall not look upon again. Longfellow was easily the greatest poet of the three, Holmes often the most brilliant and felicitous, but Lowell, in spite of his forays in politics, was the finest scholar and the most profoundly literary, as he was above the others most deeply and thoroughly New England in quality.

While I was doing these sketches, sometimes slighter and sometimes less slight, of all those poets and essayists and novelists I had known in Cambridge and Boston and Concord and New York, I was doing many other things: half a dozen novels, as many more novelettes and shorter stories, with essays and criticisms and verses; so that in January, 1900, I had not yet done the paper on Lowell, which, with another, was to complete my reminiscences of American literary life as I had witnessed it. When they were all done at last they were republished in a volume which found instant favor beyond my deserts if not its own.

There was a good deal of trouble with the name, but Literary Friends and Acquaintance was an endeavor for modest accuracy with which I remained satisfied until I thought, long too late, of Literary Friends and Neighbors. Then I perceived that this would have been still more accurate and quite as modest, and I gladly give any reader leave to call the book by that name who likes.

Since the collection was first made, I have written little else quite of the kind, except the paper on Bret Harte, which was first printed shortly after his death; and the study of Mark Twain, which I had been preparing to make for forty years and more, and wrote in two weeks of the spring of 1910. Others of my time and place have now passed whither there is neither time nor place, and there are moments when I feel that I must try to call them back and pay them such honor as my sense of their worth may give; but the impulse has as yet failed to effect itself, and I do not know how long I shall spare myself the supreme pleasure-pain, the "hochst angenehmer Schmerz," of seeking to live here with those who live here no more.

W. D. H.

LITERARY FRIENDS AND ACQUAINTANCE — My First Visit to
New England
MY FIRST VISIT TO NEW ENGLAND

If there was any one in the world who had his being more wholly
in literature than I had in 1860, I am sure I should not have known
where to find him, and I doubt if he could have been found nearer
the centres of literary activity than I then was, or among those more
purely devoted to literature than myself. I had been for three years a
writer of news paragraphs, book notices, and political leaders on a
daily paper in an inland city, and I do not know that my life dif-
fered outwardly from that of any other young journalist, who had
begun as I had in a country printing-office, and might be supposed
to be looking forward to advancement in his profession or in public
affairs. But inwardly it was altogether different with me. Inwardly I
was a poet, with no wish to be anything else, unless in a moment of
careless affluence I might so far forget myself as to be a novelist. I
was, with my friend J. J. Piatt, the half-author of a little volume of
very unknown verse, and Mr. Lowell had lately accepted and had
begun to print in the Atlantic Monthly five or six poems of mine.
Besides this I had written poems, and sketches, and criticisms for
the Saturday Press of New York, a long-forgotten but once very
lively expression of literary intention in an extinct bohemia of that
city; and I was always writing poems, and sketches, and criticisms
in our own paper. These, as well as my feats in the renowned periodicals of the East, met with kindness, if not honor, in my own city
which ought to have given me grave doubts whether I was any real
prophet. But it only intensified my literary ambition, already so
strong that my veins might well have run ink rather than blood, and
gave me a higher opinion of my fellow-citizens, if such a thing
could be. They were indeed very charming people, and such of
them as I mostly saw were readers and lovers of books. Society in
Columbus at that day had a pleasant refinement which I think I do

not exaggerate in the fond retrospect. It had the finality which it seems to have had nowhere since the war; it had certain fixed ideals, which were none the less graceful and becoming because they were the simple old American ideals, now vanished, or fast vanishing, before the knowledge of good and evil as they have it in Europe, and as it has imparted itself to American travel and sojourn. There was a mixture of many strains in the capital of Ohio, as there was throughout the State. Virginia, Kentucky, Pennsylvania, New York, and New England all joined to characterize the manners and customs. I suppose it was the South which gave the social tone; the intellectual taste among the elders was the Southern taste for the classic and the standard in literature; but we who were younger preferred the modern authors: we read Thackeray, and George Eliot, and Hawthorne, and Charles Reade, and De Quincey, and Tennyson, and Browning, and Emerson, and Longfellow, and I—I read Heine, and evermore Heine, when there was not some new thing from the others. Now and then an immediate French book penetrated to us: we read Michelet and About, I remember. We looked to England and the East largely for our literary opinions; we accepted the Saturday Review as law if we could not quite receive it as gospel. One of us took the Cornhill Magazine, because Thackeray was the editor; the Atlantic Monthly counted many readers among us; and a visiting young lady from New England, who screamed at sight of the periodical in one of our houses, "Why, have you got the Atlantic Monthly out here?" could be answered, with cold superiority, "There are several contributors to the Atlantic in Columbus." There were in fact two: my room-mate, who wrote Browning for it, while I wrote Heine and Longfellow. But I suppose two are as rightfully several as twenty are.

II.

That was the heyday of lecturing, and now and then a literary light from the East swam into our skies. I heard and saw Emerson, and I once met Bayard Taylor socially, at the hospitable house where he was a guest after his lecture. Heaven knows how I got through the evening. I do not think I opened my mouth to address him a word; it was as much as I could do to sit and look at him, while he tranquilly smoked, and chatted with our host, and quaffed the beer which we had very good in the Nest. All the while I did him homage as the first author by calling whom I had met. I longed to tell him how much I liked his poems, which we used to get by heart in those days, and I longed (how much more I longed!) to have him know that:

"Auch ich war in Arkadien geboren,"

that I had printed poems in the Atlantic Monthly and the Saturday Press, and was the potential author of things destined to eclipse all literature hitherto attempted. But I could not tell him; and there was no one else who thought to tell him. Perhaps it was as well so; I might have perished of his recognition, for my modesty was equal to my merit.

In fact I think we were all rather modest young fellows, we who formed the group wont to spend some part of every evening at that house, where there was always music, or whist, or gay talk, or all three. We had our opinions of literary matters, but (perhaps because we had mostly accepted them from England or New England, as I have said) we were not vain of them; and we would by no means have urged them before a living literary man like that. I believe none of us ventured to speak, except the poet, my roommate, who said, He believed so and so was the original of so and so; and was promptly told, He had no right to say such a thing. Naturally, we came away rather critical of our host's guest, whom I afterwards knew as the kindliest heart in the world. But we had not shone in his presence, and that galled us; and we chose to think that he had not shone in ours.

III

At that time he was filling a large space in the thoughts of the young people who had any thoughts about literature. He had come to his full repute as an agreeable and intelligent traveller, and he still wore the halo of his early adventures afoot in foreign lands when they were yet really foreign. He had not written his novels of American life, once so welcomed, and now so forgotten; it was very long before he had achieved that incomparable translation of Faust which must always remain the finest and best, and which would keep his name alive with Goethe's, if he had done nothing else worthy of remembrance. But what then most commended him to the regard of us star-eyed youth (now blinking sadly toward our seventies) was the poetry which he printed in the magazines from time to time: in the first Putnam's (where there was a dashing picture of him in an Arab burnoose and, a turban), and in Harper's, and in the Atlantic. It was often very lovely poetry, I thought, and I still think so; and it was rightfully his, though it paid the inevitable allegiance to the manner of the great masters of the day. It was graced for us by the pathetic romance of his early love, which some of its sweetest and saddest numbers confessed, for the young girl he married almost in her death hour; and we who were hoping to have our hearts broken, or already had them so, would have been glad of something more of the obvious poet in the popular lecturer we had seen refreshing himself after his hour on the platform.

He remained for nearly a year the only author I had seen, and I met him once again before I saw any other. Our second meeting was far from Columbus, as far as remote Quebec, when I was on my way to New England by way of Niagara and the Canadian rivers and cities. I stopped in Toronto, and realized myself abroad without any signal adventures; but at Montreal something very pretty happened to me. I came into the hotel office, the evening of a first day's lonely sight-seeing, and vainly explored the register for the name of some acquaintance; as I turned from it two smartly dressed young fellows embraced it, and I heard one of them say, to my great amaze and happiness, "Hello, here's Howells!"

"Oh," I broke out upon him, "I was just looking for some one I knew. I hope you are some one who knows me!"

"Only through your contributions to the Saturday Press," said the young fellow, and with these golden words, the precious first personal recognition of my authorship I had ever received from a stranger, and the rich reward of all my literary endeavor, he introduced himself and his friend. I do not know what became of this friend, or where or how he eliminated himself; but we two others were inseparable from that moment. He was a young lawyer from New York, and when I came back from Italy, four or five years later, I used to see his sign in Wall Street, with a never-fulfilled intention of going in to see him. In whatever world he happens now to be, I should like to send him my greetings, and confess to him that my art has never since brought me so sweet a recompense, and nothing a thousandth part so much like Fame, as that outcry of his over the hotel register in Montreal. We were comrades for four or five rich days, and shared our pleasures and expenses in viewing the monuments of those ancient Canadian capitals, which I think we valued at all their picturesque worth. We made jokes to mask our emotions; we giggled and made giggle, in the right way; we fell in and out of love with all the pretty faces and dresses we saw; and we talked evermore about literature and literary people. He had more acquaintance with the one, and more passion for the other, but he could tell me of Pfaff's lager-beer cellar on Broadway, where the Saturday Press fellows and the other Bohemians met; and this, for the time, was enough: I resolved to visit it as soon as I reached New York, in spite of the tobacco and beer (which I was given to understand were de rigueur), though they both, so far as I had known them, were apt to make me sick.

I was very desolate after I parted from this good fellow, who returned to Montreal on his way to New York, while I remained in Quebec to continue later on mine to New England. When I came in from seeing him off in a calash for the boat, I discovered Bayard Taylor in the reading-room, where he sat sunken in what seemed a somewhat weary muse. He did not know me, or even notice me, though I made several errands in and out of the reading-room in the vain hope that he might do so: doubly vain, for I am aware now that I was still flown with the pride of that pretty experience in Montreal, and trusted in a repetition of something like it. At last, as no chance volunteered to help me, I mustered courage to go up to him and name myself, and say I had once had the pleasure of meeting him at Doctor — — —-'s in Columbus. The poet gave no sign of consciousness at the sound of a name which I had fondly begun to think might not be so all unknown. He looked up with an unkindling eye, and asked, Ah, how was the Doctor? and when I had reported favorably of the Doctor, our conversation ended.

He was probably as tired as he looked, and he must have classed me with that multitude all over the country who had shared the pleasure I professed in meeting him before; it was surely my fault that I did not speak my name loud enough to be recognized, if I spoke it at all; but the courage I had mustered did not quite suffice for that. In after years he assured me, first by letter and then by word, of his grief for an incident which I can only recall now as the untoward beginning of a cordial friendship. It was often my privilege, in those days, as reviewer and editor, to testify my sense of the beautiful things he did in so many kinds of literature, but I never liked any of them better than I liked him. He had a fervent devotion to his art, and he was always going to do the greatest things in it, with an expectation of effect that never failed him. The things he actually did were none of them mean, or wanting in quality, and some of them are of a lasting charm that any one may feel who will turn to his poems; but no doubt many of them fell short of his hopes of them with the reader. It was fine to meet him when he was full of a new scheme; he talked of it with a single-hearted joy, and tried to make you see it of the same colors and proportions it wore to his eyes. He spared no toil to make it the perfect thing he dreamed it, and he was not discouraged by any disappointment he suffered with the critic or the public.

He was a tireless worker, and at last his health failed under his labors at the newspaper desk, beneath the midnight gas, when he should long have rested from such labors. I believe he was obliged to do them through one of those business fortuities which deform and embitter all our lives; but he was not the man to spare himself in any case. He was always attempting new things, and he never ceased endeavoring to make his scholarship reparation for the want of earlier opportunity and training. I remember that I met him once in a Cambridge street with a book in his hand which he let me take in mine. It was a Greek author, and he said he was just beginning to read the language at fifty: a patriarchal age to me of the early thirties!

I suppose I intimated the surprise I felt at his taking it up so late in the day, for he said, with charming seriousness, "Oh, but you know, I expect to use it in the other world." Yea, that made it worth while, I consented; but was he sure of the other world? "As sure as I am of this," he said; and I have always kept the impression of the young faith which spoke in his voice and was more than his words.

I saw him last in the hour of those tremendous adieux which were paid him in New York before he sailed to be minister in Germany. It was one of the most graceful things done by President Hayes, who, most of all our Presidents after Lincoln, honored himself in honoring literature by his appointments, to give that place to Bayard Taylor. There was no one more fit for it, and it was peculiarly fit that he should be so distinguished to a people who knew and valued his scholarship and the service he had done German letters. He was as happy in it, apparently, as a man could be in anything here below, and he enjoyed to the last drop the many cups of kindness pressed to his lips in parting; though I believe these farewells, at a time when he was already fagged with work and excitement, were notably harmful to him, and helped to hasten his end. Some of us who were near of friendship went down to see him off when he sailed, as the dismal and futile wont of friends is; and I recall the kind, great fellow standing in the cabin, amid those sad flowers that heaped the tables, saying good-by to one after another, and smiling fondly, smiling wearily, upon all. There was champagne, of course, and an odious hilarity, without meaning and without remission, till the warning bell chased us ashore, and our brave poet escaped with what was left of his life.

IV

I have followed him far from the moment of our first meeting; but even on my way to venerate those New England luminaries, which chiefly drew my eyes, I could not pay a less devoir to an author who, if Curtis was not, was chief of the New York group of authors in that day. I distinguished between the New-Englanders and the New-Yorkers, and I suppose there is no question but our literary centre was then in Boston, wherever it is, or is not, at present. But I thought Taylor then, and I think him now, one of the first in our whole American province of the republic of letters, in a day when it was in a recognizably flourishing state, whether we regard quantity or quality in the names that gave it lustre. Lowell was then in perfect command of those varied forces which will long, if not lastingly, keep him in memory as first among our literary men, and master in more kinds than any other American. Longfellow was in the fulness of his world-wide fame, and in the ripeness of the beautiful genius which was not to know decay while life endured. Emerson had emerged from the popular darkness which had so long held him a hopeless mystic, and was shining a lambent star of poesy and prophecy at the zenith. Hawthorne, the exquisite artist, the unrivalled dreamer, whom we still always liken this one and that one to, whenever this one or that one promises greatly to please us, and still leave without a rival, without a companion, had lately returned from his long sojourn abroad, and had given us the last of the incomparable romances which the world was to have perfect from his hand. Doctor Holmes had surpassed all expectations in those who most admired his brilliant humor and charming poetry by the invention of a new attitude if not a new sort in literature. The turn that civic affairs had taken was favorable to the widest recognition of Whittier's splendid lyrical gift; and that heart of fire, doubly snow-bound by Quaker tradition and Puritan environment; was penetrating every generous breast with its flamy impulses, and fusing all wills in its noble purpose. Mrs. Stowe, who far outfamed the rest as the author of the most renowned novel ever written, was proving it no accident or miracle by the fiction she was still writing.

This great New England group might be enlarged perhaps without loss of quality by the inclusion of Thoreau, who came somewhat before his time, and whose drastic criticism of our expediential and mainly futile civilization would find more intelligent acceptance now than it did then, when all resentment of its defects was specialized in enmity to Southern slavery. Doctor Edward Everett Hale belonged in this group too, by virtue of that humor, the most inventive and the most fantastic, the sanest, the sweetest, the truest, which had begun to find expression in the Atlantic Monthly; and there a wonderful young girl had written a series of vivid sketches and taken the heart of youth everywhere with amaze and joy, so that I thought it would be no less an event to meet Harriet Prescott than to meet any of those I have named.

I expected somehow to meet them all, and I imagined them all easily accessible in the office of the Atlantic Monthly, which had lately adventured in the fine air of high literature where so many other periodicals had gasped and died before it. The best of these, hitherto, and better even than the Atlantic for some reasons, the lamented Putnam's Magazine, had perished of inanition at New York, and the claim of the commercial capital to the literary primacy had passed with that brilliant venture. New York had nothing distinctive to show for American literature but the decrepit and doting Knickerbocker Magazine. Harper's New Monthly, though Curtis had already come to it from the wreck of Putnam's, and it had long ceased to be eclectic in material, and had begun to stand for native work in the allied arts which it has since so magnificently advanced, was not distinctively literary, and the Weekly had just begun to make itself known. The Century, Scribner's, the Cosmopolitan, McClure's, and I know not what others, were still unimagined by five, and ten, and twenty years, and the Galaxy was to flash and fade before any of them should kindle its more effectual fires. The Nation, which was destined to chastise rather than nurture our young literature, had still six years of dreamless potentiality before it; and the Nation was always more Bostonian than New-Yorkish by nature, whatever it was by nativity.

Philadelphia had long counted for nothing in the literary field. Graham's Magazine at one time showed a certain critical force, but it seemed to perish of this expression of vitality; and there remained Godey's Lady's Book and Peterson's Magazine, publications really incredible in their insipidity. In the South there was nothing but a mistaken social ideal, with the moral principles all standing on their heads in defence of slavery; and in the West there was a feeble and foolish notion that Western talent was repressed by Eastern jealousy. At Boston chiefly, if not at Boston alone, was there a vigorous intellectual life among such authors as I have named. Every young writer was ambitious to join his name with theirs in the Atlantic Monthly, and in the lists of Ticknor & Fields, who were literary publishers in a sense such as the business world has known nowhere else before or since. Their imprint was a warrant of quality to the reader and of immortality to the author, so that if I could have had a book issued by them at that day I should now be in the full enjoyment of an undying fame.

V.

Such was the literary situation as the passionate pilgrim from the West approached his holy land at Boston, by way of the Grand Trunk Railway from Quebec to Portland. I have no recollection of a sleeping-car, and I suppose I waked and watched during the whole of that long, rough journey; but I should hardly have slept if there had been a car for the purpose. I was too eager to see what New England was like, and too anxious not to lose the least glimpse of it, to close my eyes after I crossed the border at Island Pond. I found that in the elm-dotted levels of Maine it was very like the Western Reserve in northern Ohio, which is, indeed, a portion of New England transferred with all its characteristic features, and flattened out along the lake shore. It was not till I began to run southward into the older regions of the country that it lost this look, and became gratefully strange to me. It never had the effect of hoary antiquity which I had expected of a country settled more than two centuries; with its wood-built farms and villages it looked newer than the coal-smoked brick of southern Ohio. I had prefigured the New England landscape bare of forests, relieved here and there with the tees of orchards or plantations; but I found apparently as much woodland as at home.

At Portland I first saw the ocean, and this was a sort of disappointment. Tides and salt water I had already had at Quebec, so that I was no longer on the alert for them; but the color and the vastness of the sea I was still to try upon my vision. When I stood on the Promenade at Portland with the kind young Unitarian minister whom I had brought a letter to, and who led me there for a most impressive first view of the ocean, I could not make more of it than there was of Lake Erie; and I have never thought the color of the sea comparable to the tender blue of the lake. I did not hint my disappointment to my friend; I had too much regard for the feelings of an Eastern man to decry his ocean to his face, and I felt besides that it would be vulgar and provincial to make comparisons. I am glad now that I held my tongue, for that kind soul is no longer in this world, and I should not like to think he knew how far short of my expectations the sea he was so proud of had fallen. I went up with him into a tower or belvedere there was at hand; and when he pointed to the eastern horizon and said, Now there was nothing but sea between us and Africa, I pretended to expand with the thought, and began to sound myself for the emotions which I ought to have felt at such a sight. But in my heart I was empty, and Heaven knows whether I saw the steamer which the ancient mariner in charge of that tower invited me to look at through his telescope. I never could see anything but a vitreous glare through a telescope, which has a vicious habit of dodging about through space, and failing to bring down anything of less than planetary magnitude.

But there was something at Portland vastly more to me than seas or continents, and that was the house where Longfellow was born. I believe, now, I did not get the right house, but only the house he went to live in later; but it served, and I rejoiced in it with a rapture that could not have been more genuine if it had been the real birth-place of the poet. I got my friend to show me

> "——the breezy dome of groves,
> The shadows of Deering's woods,"

because they were in one of Longfellow's loveliest and tenderest poems; and I made an errand to the docks, for the sake of the

> "—-black wharves and the slips,
> And the sea-tides tossing free,
> And Spanish sailors with bearded lips,
> And the beauty and mystery of the ships,
> And the magic of the sea,"

mainly for the reason that these were colors and shapes of the fond vision of the poet's past. I am in doubt whether it was at this time or a later time that I went to revere

> "—the dead captains as they lay
> In their graves o'erlooking the tranquil bay,
> where they in battle died,"

but I am quite sure it was now that I wandered under

> "— the trees which shadow each well-
> known street, As they balance up and
> down,"

for when I was next in Portland the great fire had swept the city avenues bare of most of those beautiful elms, whose Gothic arches and traceries I well remember.

The fact is that in those days I was bursting with the most romantic expectations of life in every way, and I looked at the whole world as material that might be turned into literature, or that might be associated with it somehow. I do not know how I managed to keep these preposterous hopes within me, but perhaps the trick of satirizing them, which I had early learnt, helped me to do it. I was at that particular moment resolved above all things to see things as Heinrich Heine saw them, or at least to report them as he did, no matter how I saw them; and I went about framing phrases to this end, and trying to match the objects of interest to them whenever there was the least chance of getting them together.

VI.

I do not know how I first arrived in Boston, or whether it was before or after I had passed a day or two in Salem. As Salem is on the way from Portland, I will suppose that I stopped there first, and explored the quaint old town (quainter then than now, but still quaint enough) for the memorials of Hawthorne and of the witches which united to form the Salem I cared for. I went and looked up the House of Seven Gables, and suffered an unreasonable disappointment that it had not a great many more of them; but there was no loss in the death-warrant of Bridget Bishop, with the sheriff's return of execution upon it, which I found at the Court-house; if anything, the pathos of that witness of one of the cruelest delusions in the world was rather in excess of my needs; I could have got on with less. I saw the pins which the witches were sworn to have thrust into the afflicted children, and I saw Gallows Hill, where the hapless victims of the perjury were hanged. But that death-warrant remained the most vivid color of my experience of the tragedy; I had no need to invite myself to a sense of it, and it is still like a stain of red in my memory.

The kind old ship's captain whose guest I was, and who was transfigured to poetry in my sense by the fact that he used to voyage to the African coast for palm-oil in former days, led me all about the town, and showed me the Custom-house, which I desired to see because it was in the preface to the Scarlet Letter. But I perceived that he did not share my enthusiasm for the author, and I became more and more sensible that in Salem air there was a cool undercurrent of feeling about him. No doubt the place was not altogether grateful for the celebrity his romance had given it, and would have valued more the uninterrupted quiet of its own flattering thoughts of itself; but when it came to hearing a young lady say she knew a girl who said she would like to poison Hawthorne, it seemed to the devout young pilgrim from the West that something more of love for the great romancer would not have been too much for him. Hawthorne had already had his say, however, and he had not used his native town with any great tenderness. Indeed, the advantages to any place of having a great genius born and reared in its midst are so doubtful that it might be well for localities designing to become the birthplaces of distinguished authors to think twice about it. Perhaps only the largest capitals, like London and Paris, and New York and Chicago, ought to risk it. But the authors have an unaccountable perversity, and will seldom come into the world in the large cities, which are alone without the sense of neighborhood, and the personal susceptibilities so unfavorable to the practice of the literary art. I dare say that it was owing to the local indifference to her greatest name, or her reluctance from it, that I got a clearer impression of Salem in some other respects than I should have had if I had been invited there to devote myself solely to the associations of Hawthorne. For the first time I saw an old New England town, I do not know, but the most characteristic, and took into my young Western consciousness the fact of a more complex civilization than I had yet known. My whole life had been passed in a region where men were just beginning ancestors, and the conception of family was very imperfect. Literature, of course, was full of it, and it was not for a devotee of Thackeray to be theoretically ignorant of its manifestations; but I had hitherto carelessly supposed that family was nowhere regarded seriously in America except in Virginia, where it furnished a joke for the rest of the nation. But now I found myself confronted with it in its ancient houses, and heard its names pronounced with a certain consideration, which I dare say was as much their due in Salem as it could be anywhere. The names were all strange, and all indifferent to me, but those fine square wooden mansions, of a tasteful architecture, and a pale buff-color, withdrawing themselves in quiet reserve from the quiet street, gave me an impression of family as an actuality and a force which I had never had before, but which no Westerner can yet understand the East without taking into account. I do not suppose that I conceived of family as a fact of vital import then; I think I rather regarded it as a color to be used in any aesthetic study of the local conditions. I am not sure that I valued it more even for literary purposes, than the steeple which the captain pointed out as the first and last thing he saw when he came and went on his long voyages, or than the great palm-oil casks, which he showed me, and which I related to the tree that stood

"Auf brennender Felsenwand."

Whether that was the kind of palm that gives the oil, or was a sort only suitable to be the dream of a lonely fir-tree in the North on a cold height, I am in doubt to this day.

I heard, not without concern, that the neighboring industry of Lynn was penetrating Salem, and that the ancient haunt of the witches and the birthplace of our subtlest and somberest wizard was becoming a great shoe-town; but my concern was less for its memories and sensibilities than for an odious duty which I owed that industry, together with all the others in New England. Before I left home I had promised my earliest publisher that I would undertake to edit, or compile, or do something literary to, a work on the operation of the more distinctive mechanical inventions of our country, which he had conceived the notion of publishing by subscription. He had furnished me, the most immechanical of humankind, with a letter addressed generally to the great mills and factories of the East, entreating their managers to unfold their mysteries to me for the purposes of this volume. His letter had the effect of shutting up some of them like clams, and others it put upon their guard against my researches, lest I should seize the secret of their special inventions and publish it to the world. I could not tell the managers that I was both morally and mentally incapable of this; that they might have explained and demonstrated the properties and functions of their most recondite machinery, and upon examination afterwards found me guiltless of having anything but a few verses of Heine or Tennyson or Longfellow in my head. So I had to suffer in several places from their unjust anxieties, and from my own weariness of their ingenious engines, or else endure the pangs of a bad conscience from ignoring them. As long as I was in Canada I was happy, for there was no industry in Canada that I saw, except that of the peasant girls, in their Evangeline hats and kirtles, tossing the hay in the way-side fields; but when I reached Portland my troubles began. I went with that young minister of whom I have spoken to a large foundry, where they were casting some sort of ironmongery, and inspected the process from a distance beyond any chance spurt of the molten metal, and came away sadly uncertain of putting the rather fine spectacle to any practical use. A manufactory where they did something with coal-oil (which I now heard for the first time called kerosene) refused itself to me, and I said to myself that probably all the other industries of Portland were as reserved, and I would not seek to explore them; but when I got to Salem, my conscience stirred again. If I knew that there were shoe-shops in Salem, ought not I to go and inspect their processes? This was a question which would not answer itself to my satisfaction, and I had no peace till I learned that I could see shoemaking much better at Lynn, and that Lynn was such a little way from Boston that I could readily run up there, if I did not wish to examine the shoe machinery at once. I promised myself that I would run up from Boston, but in order to do this I must first go to Boston.

VII.

I am supposing still that I saw Salem before I saw Boston, but however the fact may be, I am sure that I decided it would be better to see shoemaking in Lynn, where I really did see it, thirty years later. For the purposes of the present visit, I contented myself with looking at a machine in Haverhill, which chewed a shoe sole full of pegs, and dropped it out of its iron jaws with an indifference as great as my own, and probably as little sense of how it had done its work. I may be unjust to that machine; Heaven knows I would not wrong it; and I must confess that my head had no room in it for the conception of any machinery but the mythological, which also I despised, in my revulsion from the eighteenth-century poets to those of my own day.

I cannot quite make out after the lapse of so many years just how or when I got to Haverhill, or whether it was before or after I had been in Salem. There is an apparitional quality in my presences, at this point or that, in the dim past; but I hope that, for the credit of their order, ghosts are not commonly taken with such trivial things as I was. For instance, in Haverhill I was much interested by the sight of a young man, coming gayly down the steps of the hotel where I lodged, in peg-top trousers so much more peg top than my own that I seemed to be wearing mere spring-bottoms in comparison; and in a day when every one who respected himself had a necktie as narrow as he could get, this youth had one no wider than a shoestring, and red at that, while mine measured almost an inch, and was black. To be sure, he was one of a band of negro minstrels, who were to give a concert that night, and he had a light to excel in fashion.

I will suppose, for convenience' sake, that I visited Haverhill, too, before I reached Boston: somehow that shoe-pegging machine must come in, and it may as well come in here. When I actually found myself in Boston, there were perhaps industries which it would have been well for me to celebrate, but I either made believe there were none, or else I honestly forgot all about them. In either case I released myself altogether to the literary and historical associations of the place. I need not say that I gave myself first to the first, and it rather surprised me to find that the literary associations of Boston referred so largely to Cambridge. I did not know much about Cambridge, except that it was the seat of the university where Lowell was, and Longfellow had been, professor; and somehow I had not realized it as the home of these poets. That was rather stupid of me, but it is best to own the truth, and afterward I came to know the place so well that I may safely confess my earlier ignorance.

I had stopped in Boston at the Tremont House, which was still one of the first hostelries of the country, and I must have inquired my way to Cambridge there; but I was sceptical of the direction the Cambridge horse-car took when I found it, and I hinted to the driver my anxieties as to why he should be starting east when I had been told that Cambridge was west of Boston. He reassured me in the laconic and sarcastic manner of his kind, and we really reached Cambridge by the route he had taken.

The beautiful elms that shaded great part of the way massed themselves in the "groves of academe" at the Square, and showed pleasant glimpses of "Old Harvard's scholar factories red," then far fewer than now. It must have been in vacation, for I met no one as I wandered through the college yard, trying to make up my mind as to how I should learn where Lowell lived; for it was he whom I had come to find. He had not only taken the poems I sent him, but he had printed two of them in a single number of the Atlantic, and had even written me a little note about them, which I wore next my heart in my breast pocket till I almost wore it out; and so I thought I might fitly report myself to him. But I have always been helpless in finding my way, and I was still depressed by my failure to convince the horse-car driver that he had taken the wrong road. I let several people go by without questioning them, and those I did ask abashed me farther by not knowing what I wanted to know. When I had remitted my search for the moment, an ancient man, with an open mouth and an inquiring eye, whom I never afterwards made out in Cambridge, addressed me with a hospitable offer to show me the Washington Elm. I thought this would give me time to embolden myself for the meeting with the editor of the Atlantic if I should ever find him, and I went with that kind old man, who when he had shown me the tree, and the spot where Washington stood when he took command of the Continental forces, said that he had a branch of it, and that if I would come to his house with him he would give me a piece. In the end, I meant merely to flatter him into telling me where I could find Lowell, but I dissembled my purpose and pretended a passion for a piece of the historic elm, and the old man led me not only to his house but his wood-house, where he sawed me off a block so generous that I could not get it into my pocket. I feigned the gratitude which I could see that he expected, and then I took courage to put my question to him. Perhaps that patriarch lived only in the past, and cared for history and not literature. He confessed that he could not tell me where to find Lowell; but he did not forsake me; he set forth with me upon the street again, and let no man pass without asking him. In the end we met one who was able to say where Mr. Lowell was, and I found him at last in a little study at the rear of a pleasant, old-fashioned house near the Delta.

Lowell was not then at the height of his fame; he had just reached this thirty years after, when he died; but I doubt if he was ever after a greater power in his own country, or more completely embodied the literary aspiration which would not and could not part itself from the love of freedom and the hope of justice. For the sake of these he had been willing to suffer the reproach which followed their friends in the earlier days of the anti-slavery struggle: He had outlived the reproach long before; but the fear of his strength remained with those who had felt it, and he had not made himself more generally loved by the 'Fable for Critics' than by the 'Biglow Papers', probably. But in the 'Vision of Sir Launfal' and the 'Legend of Brittany' he had won a liking if not a listening far wider than his humor and his wit had got him; and in his lectures on the English poets, given not many years before he came to the charge of the Atlantic, he had proved himself easily the wisest and finest critic in our language. He was already, more than any American poet,

"Dowered with the hate of hate, the scorn of scorn,
    The love of love,"

and he held a place in the public sense which no other author among us has held. I had myself never been a great reader of his poetry, when I met him, though when I was a boy of ten years I had heard my father repeat passages from the Biglow Papers against war and slavery and the war for slavery upon Mexico, and later I had read those criticisms of English poetry, and I knew Sir Launfal must be Lowell in some sort; but my love for him as a poet was chiefly centred in my love for his tender rhyme, 'Auf Wiedersehen', which I can not yet read without something of the young pathos it first stirred in me. I knew and felt his greatness some how apart from the literary proofs of it; he ruled my fancy and held my allegiance as a character, as a man; and I am neither sorry nor ashamed that I was abashed when I first came into his presence; and that in spite of his words of welcome I sat inwardly quaking before him. He was then forty-one years old, and nineteen my senior, and if there had been nothing else to awe me, I might well have been quelled by the disparity of our ages. But I have always been willing and even eager to do homage to men who have done something, and notably to men who have done something in the sort I wished to do something in, myself. I could never recognize any other sort of superiority; but that I am proud to recognize; and I had before Lowell some such feeling as an obscure subaltern might have before his general. He was by nature a bit of a disciplinarian, and the effect was from him as well as in me; I dare say he let me feel whatever difference there was as helplessly as I felt it. At the first encounter with people he always was apt to have a certain frosty shyness, a smiling cold, as from the long, high-sunned winters of his Puritan race; he was not quite himself till he had made you aware of his quality: then no one could be sweeter, tenderer, warmer than he; then he made you free of his whole heart; but you must be his captive before he could do that. His whole personality had now an instant charm for me; I could not keep my eyes from those beautiful eyes of his, which had a certain starry serenity, and looked out so purely from under his white forehead, shadowed with auburn hair untouched by age; or from the smile that shaped the auburn beard, and gave the face in its form and color the Christ-look which Page's portrait has flattered in it.

His voice had as great a fascination for me as his face. The vibrant tenderness and the crisp clearness of the tones, the perfect modulation, the clear enunciation, the exquisite accent, the elect diction—I did not know enough then to know that these were the gifts, these were the graces, of one from whose tongue our rough English came music such as I should never hear from any other. In this speech there was nothing of our slipshod American slovenliness, but a truly Italian conscience and an artistic sense of beauty in the instrument.

I saw, before he sat down across his writing-table from me, that he was not far from the medium height; but his erect carriage made the most of his five feet and odd inches. He had been smoking the pipe he loved, and he put it back in his mouth, presently, as if he found himself at greater ease with it, when he began to chat, or rather to let me show what manner of young man I was by giving me the first word. I told him of the trouble I had in finding him, and I could not help dragging in something about Heine's search for Borne, when he went to see him in Frankfort; but I felt at once this was a false start, for Lowell was such an impassioned lover of Cambridge, which was truly his patria, in the Italian sense, that it must have hurt him to be unknown to any one in it; he said, a little dryly, that he should not have thought I would have so much difficulty; but he added, forgivingly, that this was not his own house, which he was out of for the time. Then he spoke to me of Heine, and when I showed my ardor for him, he sought to temper it with some judicious criticisms, and told me that he had kept the first poem I sent him, for the long time it had been unacknowledged, to make sure that it was not a translation. He asked me about myself, and my name, and its Welsh origin, and seemed to find the vanity I had in this harmless enough. When I said I had tried hard to believe that I was at least the literary descendant of Sir James Howels, he corrected me gently with "James Howel," and took down a volume of the 'Familiar Letters' from the shelves behind him to prove me wrong. This was always his habit, as I found afterwards when he quoted anything from a book he liked to get it and read the passage over, as if he tasted a kind of hoarded sweetness in the words. It visibly vexed him if they showed him in the least mistaken; but

"The love he bore to learning was at fault"

for this foible, and that other of setting people right if he thought them wrong. I could not assert myself against his version of Howels's name, for my edition of his letters was far away in Ohio, and I was obliged to own that the name was spelt in several different ways in it. He perceived, no doubt, why I had chosen the form liked my own, with the title which the pleasant old turncoat ought to have had from the many masters he served according to their many minds, but never had except from that erring edition. He did not afflict me for it, though; probably it amused him too much; he asked me about the West, and when he found that I was as proud of the West as I was of Wales, he seemed even better pleased, and said he had always fancied that human nature was laid out on rather a larger scale there than in the East, but he had seen very little of the West. In my heart I did not think this then, and I do not think it now; human nature has had more ground to spread over in the West; that is all; but "it was not for me to bandy words with my sovereign." He said he liked to hear of the differences between the different sections, for what we had most to fear in our country was a wearisome sameness of type.

He did not say now, or at any other time during the many years I knew him, any of those slighting things of the West which I had so often to suffer from Eastern people, but suffered me to praise it all I would. He asked me what way I had taken in coming to New England, and when I told him, and began to rave of the beauty and quaintness of French Canada, and to pour out my joy in Quebec, he said, with a smile that had now lost all its frost, Yes, Quebec was a bit of the seventeenth century; it was in many ways more French than France, and its people spoke the language of Voltaire, with the accent of Voltaire's time.

I do not remember what else he talked of, though once I remembered it with what I believed an ineffaceable distinctness. I set nothing of it down at the time; I was too busy with the letters I was writing for a Cincinnati paper; and I was severely bent upon keeping all personalities out of them. This was very well, but I could wish now that I had transgressed at least so far as to report some of the things that Lowell said; for the paper did not print my letters, and it would have been perfectly safe, and very useful for the present purpose. But perhaps he did not say anything very memorable; to do that you must have something positive in your listener; and I was the mere response, the hollow echo, that youth must be in like circumstances. I was all the time afraid of wearing my welcome out, and I hurried to go when I would so gladly have staid. I do not remember where I meant to go, or why he should have undertaken to show me the way across-lots, but this was what he did; and when we came to a fence, which I clambered gracelessly over, he put his hands on the top, and tried to take it at a bound. He tried twice, and then laughed at his failure, but not with any great pleasure, and he was not content till a third trial carried him across. Then he said, "I commonly do that the first time," as if it were a frequent habit with him, while I remained discreetly silent, and for that moment at least felt myself the elder of the man who had so much of the boy in him. He had, indeed, much of the boy in him to the last, and he parted with each hour of his youth reluctantly, pathetically.

VIII.

We walked across what must have been Jarvis Field to what must have been North Avenue, and there he left me. But before he let me go he held my hand while he could say that he wished me to dine with him; only, he was not in his own house, and he would ask me to dine with him at the Parker House in Boston, and would send me word of the time later.

I suppose I may have spent part of the intervening time in viewing the wonders of Boston, and visiting the historic scenes and places in it and about it. I certainly went over to Charleston, and ascended Bunker Hill monument, and explored the navy-yard, where the immemorial man-of-war begun in Jackson's time was then silently stretching itself under its long shed in a poetic arrest, as if the failure of the appropriation for its completion had been some kind of enchantment. In Boston, I early presented my letter of credit to the publisher it was drawn upon, not that I needed money at the moment, but from a young eagerness to see if it would be honored; and a literary attache of the house kindly went about with me, and showed me the life of the city. A great city it seemed to me then, and a seething vortex of business as well as a whirl of gaiety, as I saw it in Washington Street, and in a promenade concert at Copeland's restaurant in Tremont Row. Probably I brought some idealizing force to bear upon it, for I was not all so strange to the world as I must seem; perhaps I accounted for quality as well as quantity in my impressions of the New England metropolis, and aggrandized it in the ratio of its literary importance. It seemed to me old, even after Quebec, and very likely I credited the actual town with all the dead and gone Bostonians in my sentimental census. If I did not, it was no fault of my cicerone, who thought even more of the city he showed me than I did. I do not know now who he was, and I never saw him after I came to live there, with any certainty that it was he, though I was often tormented with the vision of a spectacled face like his, but not like enough to warrant me in addressing him.

He became part of that ghostly Boston of my first visit, which would sometimes return and possess again the city I came to know so familiarly in later years, and to be so passionately interested in. Some color of my prime impressions has tinged the fictitious experiences of people in my books, but I find very little of it in my memory. This is like a web of frayed old lace, which I have to take carefully into my hold for fear of its fragility, and make out as best I can the figure once so distinct in it. There are the narrow streets, stretching saltworks to the docks, which I haunted for their quaintness, and there is Faunal Hall, which I cared to see so much more because Wendell Phillips had spoken in it than because Otis and Adams had. There is the old Colonial House, and there is the State House, which I dare say I explored, with the Common sloping before it. There is Beacon Street, with the Hancock House where it is incredibly no more, and there are the beginnings of Commonwealth Avenue, and the other streets of the Back Bay, laid out with their basements left hollowed in the made land, which the gravel trains were yet making out of the westward hills. There is the Public Garden, newly planned and planted, but without the massive bridge destined to make so ungratefully little of the lake that occasioned it. But it is all very vague, and I could easily believe now that it was some one else who saw it then in my place.

I think that I did not try to see Cambridge the same day that I saw Lowell, but wisely came back to my hotel in Boston, and tried to realize the fact. I went out another day, with an acquaintance from Ohio; whom I ran upon in the street. We went to Mount Auburn together, and I viewed its monuments with a reverence which I dare say their artistic quality did not merit. But I am, not sorry for this, for perhaps they are not quite so bad as some people pretend. The Gothic chapel of the cemetery, unsorted as it was, gave me, with its half-dozen statues standing or sitting about, an emotion such as I am afraid I could not receive now from the Acropolis, Westminster Abbey, and Santa Crocea in one. I tried hard for some aesthetic sense of it, and I made believe that I thought this thing and that thing in the place moved me with its fitness or beauty; but the truth is that I had no taste in anything but literature, and did not feel the effect I would so willingly have experienced.

I did genuinely love the elmy quiet of the dear old Cambridge streets, though, and I had a real and instant pleasure in the yellow colonial houses, with their white corners and casements and their green blinds, that lurked behind the shrubbery of the avenue I passed through to Mount Auburn. The most beautiful among them was the most interesting for me, for it was the house of Longfellow; my companion, who had seen it before, pointed it out to me with an air of custom, and I would not let him see that I valued the first sight of it as I did. I had hoped that somehow I might be so favored as to see Longfellow himself, but when I asked about him of those who knew, they said, "Oh, he is at Nahant," and I thought that Nahant must be a great way off, and at any rate I did not feel authorized to go to him there. Neither did I go to see the author of 'The Amber Gods' who lived at Newburyport, I was told, as if I should know where Newburyport was; I did not know, and I hated to ask. Besides, it did not seem so simple as it had seemed in Ohio, to go and see a young lady simply because I was infatuated with her literature; even as the envoy of all the infatuated young people of Columbus, I could not quite do this; and when I got home, I had to account for my failure as best I could. Another failure of mine was the sight of Whittier, which I then very much longed to have. They said, "Oh, Whittier lives at Amesbury," but that put him at an indefinite distance, and without the introduction I never would ask for, I found it impossible to set out in quest of him. In the end, I saw no one in New England whom I was not presented to in the regular way, except Lowell, whom I thought I had a right to call upon in my quality of contributor, and from the acquaintance I had with him by letter. I neither praise nor blame myself for this; it was my shyness that with held me rather than my merit. There is really no harm in seeking the presence of a famous man, and I doubt if the famous man resents the wish of people to look upon him without some measure, great or little, of affectation. There are bores everywhere, but he is likelier to find them in the wonted figures of society than in those young people, or old people, who come to him in the love of what he has done. I am well aware how furiously Tennyson sometimes met his worshippers, and how insolently Carlyle, but I think these facts are little specks in their sincerity. Our own gentler and honester celebrities did not forbid approach, and I have known some of them caress adorers who seemed hardly worthy of their kindness; but that was better than to have hurt any sensitive spirit who had ventured too far, by the rules that govern us with common men.

IX.

My business relations were with the house that so promptly honored my letter of credit. This house had published in the East the campaign life of Lincoln which I had lately written, and I dare say would have published the volume of poems I had written earlier with my friend Piatt, if there had been any public for it; at least, I saw large numbers of the book on the counters. But all my literary affiliations were with Ticknor & Fields, and it was the Old Corner Book-Store on Washington Street that drew my heart as soon as I had replenished my pocket in Cornhill. After verifying the editor of the Atlantic Monthly I wised to verify its publishers, and it very fitly happened that when I was shown into Mr. Fields's little room at the back of the store, with its window looking upon School Street, and its scholarly keeping in books and prints, he had just got the magazine sheets of a poem of mine from the Cambridge printers. He was then lately from abroad, and he had the zest for American things which a foreign sojourn is apt to renew in us, though I did not know this then, and could not account for it in the kindness he expressed for my poem. He introduced me to Mr. Ticknor, who I fancied had not read my poem; but he seemed to know what it was from the junior partner, and he asked me whether I had been paid for it. I confessed that I had not, and then he got out a chamois-leather bag, and took from it five half-eagles in gold and laid them on the green cloth top of the desk, in much the shape and of much the size of the Great Bear. I have never since felt myself paid so lavishly for any literary work, though I have had more for a single piece than the twenty-five dollars that dazzled me in this constellation. The publisher seemed aware of the poetic character of the transaction; he let the pieces lie a moment, before he gathered them up and put them into my hand, and said, "I always think it is pleasant to have it in gold."

But a terrible experience with the poem awaited me, and quenched for the moment all my pleasure and pride. It was 'The Pilot's Story,' which I suppose has had as much acceptance as anything of mine in verse (I do not boast of a vast acceptance for it), and I had attempted to treat in it a phase of the national tragedy of slavery, as I had imagined it on a Mississippi steamboat. A young planter has gambled away the slave-girl who is the mother of his child, and when he tells her, she breaks out upon him with the demand:

"What will you say to our boy when he cries for me, there in Saint Louis?"

I had thought this very well, and natural and simple, but a fatal proof-reader had not thought it well enough, or simple and natural enough, and he had made the line read:

"What will you say to our boy when he cries for 'Ma,' there in Saint
  Louis?"

He had even had the inspiration to quote the word he preferred to the one I had written, so that there was no merciful possibility of mistaking it for a misprint, and my blood froze in my veins at sight of it. Mr. Fields had given me the sheets to read while he looked over some letters, and he either felt the chill of my horror, or I made some sign or sound of dismay that caught his notice, for he looked round at me. I could only show him the passage with a gasp. I dare say he might have liked to laugh, for it was cruelly funny, but he did not; he was concerned for the magazine as well as for me. He declared that when he first read the line he had thought I could not have written it so, and he agreed with me that it would kill the poem if it came out in that shape. He instantly set about repairing the mischief, so far as could be. He found that the whole edition of that sheet had been printed, and the air blackened round me again, lighted up here and there with baleful flashes of the newspaper wit at my cost, which I previsioned in my misery; I knew what I should have said of such a thing myself, if it had been another's. But the publisher at once decided that the sheet must be reprinted, and I went away weak as if in the escape from some deadly peril. Afterwards it appeared that the line had passed the first proof-reader as I wrote it, but that the final reader had entered so sympathetically

into the realistic intention of my poem as to contribute the modifica-
tion which had nearly been my end.

X.

As it fell out, I lived without farther difficulty to the day and hour of the dinner Lowell made for me; and I really think, looking at myself impersonally, and remembering the sort of young fellow I was, that it would have been a great pity if I had not. The dinner was at the old-fashioned Boston hour of two, and the table was laid for four people in some little upper room at Parker's, which I was never afterwards able to make sure of. Lowell was already, there when I came, and he presented me, to my inexpressible delight and surprise, to Dr. Holmes, who was there with him.

Holmes was in the most brilliant hour of that wonderful second youth which his fame flowered into long after the world thought he had completed the cycle of his literary life. He had already received full recognition as a poet of delicate wit, nimble humor, airy imagination, and exquisite grace, when the Autocrat papers advanced his name indefinitely beyond the bounds which most immortals would have found range enough. The marvel of his invention was still fresh in the minds of men, and time had not dulled in any measure the sense of its novelty. His readers all fondly identified him with his work; and I fully expected to find myself in the Autocrat's presence when I met Dr. Holmes. But the fascination was none the less for that reason; and the winning smile, the wise and humorous glance, the whole genial manner was as important to me as if I had foreboded something altogether different. I found him physically of the Napoleonic height which spiritually overtops the Alps, and I could look into his face without that unpleasant effort which giants of inferior mind so often cost the man of five feet four.

A little while after, Fields came in, and then our number and my pleasure were complete.

Nothing else so richly satisfactory, indeed, as the whole affair could have happened to a like youth at such a point in his career; and when I sat down with Doctor Holmes and Mr. Fields, on Lowell's right, I felt through and through the dramatic perfection of the event. The kindly Autocrat recognized some such quality of it in terms which were not the less precious and gracious for their humorous excess. I have no reason to think that he had yet read any of my poor verses, or had me otherwise than wholly on trust from Lowell; but he leaned over towards his host, and said, with a laughing look at me, "Well, James, this is something like the apostolic succession; this is the laying on of hands." I took his sweet and caressing irony as he meant it; but the charm of it went to my head long before any drop of wine, together with the charm of hearing him and Lowell calling each other James and Wendell, and of finding them still cordially boys together.

I would gladly have glimmered before those great lights in the talk that followed, if I could have thought of anything brilliant to say, but I could not, and so I let them shine without a ray of reflected splendor from me. It was such talk as I had, of course, never heard before, and it is not saying enough to say that I have never heard such talk since except from these two men. It was as light and kind as it was deep and true, and it ranged over a hundred things, with a perpetual sparkle of Doctor Holmes's wit, and the constant glow of Lowell's incandescent sense. From time to time Fields came in with one of his delightful stories (sketches of character they were, which he sometimes did not mind caricaturing), or with some criticism of the literary situation from his stand-point of both lover and publisher of books. I heard fames that I had accepted as proofs of power treated as factitious, and witnessed a frankness concerning authorship, far and near, that I had not dreamed of authors using. When Doctor Holmes understood that I wrote for the 'Saturday Press', which was running amuck among some Bostonian immortalities of the day, he seemed willing that I should know they were not thought so very undying in Boston, and that I should not take the notion of a Mutual Admiration Society too seriously, or accept the New York Bohemian view of Boston as true. For the most part the talk did not address itself to me, but became an exchange of thoughts and fancies between himself and Lowell. They touched, I remember, on certain matters of technique, and the doctor confessed that he had a prejudice against some words that he could not overcome; for instance, he said, nothing could induce him to use 'neath for beneath, no exigency of versification or stress of rhyme.

Lowell contended that he would use any word that carried his meaning; and I think he did this to the hurt of some of his earlier things. He was then probably in the revolt against too much literature in literature, which every one is destined sooner or later to share; there was a certain roughness, very like crudeness, which he indulged before his thought and phrase mellowed to one music in his later work. I tacitly agreed rather with the doctor, though I did not swerve from my allegiance to Lowell, and if I had spoken I should have sided with him: I would have given that or any other proof of my devotion. Fields casually mentioned that he thought "The Dandelion" was the most popularly liked of Lowell's briefer poems, and I made haste to say that I thought so too, though I did not really think anything about it; and then I was sorry, for I could see that the poet did not like it, quite; and I felt that I was duly punished for my dishonesty.

Hawthorne was named among other authors, probably by Fields, whose house had just published his "Marble Faun," and who had recently come home on the same steamer with him. Doctor Holmes asked if I had met Hawthorne yet, and when I confessed that I had hardly yet even hoped for such a thing, he smiled his winning smile, and said: "Ah, well! I don't know that you will ever feel you have really met him. He is like a dim room with a little taper of personality burning on the corner of the mantel."

They all spoke of Hawthorne, and with the same affection, but the same sense of something mystical and remote in him; and every word was priceless to me. But these masters of the craft I was 'prentice to probably could not have said anything that I should not have found wise and well, and I am sure now I should have been the loser if the talk had shunned any of the phases of human nature which it touched. It is best to find that all men are of the same make, and that there are certain universal things which interest them as much as the supernal things, and amuse them even more. There was a saying of Lowell's which he was fond of repeating at the menace of any form of the transcendental, and he liked to warn himself and others with his homely, "Remember the dinner-bell." What I recall of the whole effect of a time so happy for me is that in all that was said, however high, however fine, we were never out of hearing of the dinner-bell; and perhaps this is the best effect I can leave with the reader. It was the first dinner served in courses that I had sat down to, and I felt that this service gave it a romantic importance which the older fashion of the West still wanted. Even at Governor Chase's table in Columbus the Governor carved; I knew of the dinner 'a la Russe', as it was then called, only from books; and it was a sort of literary flavor that I tasted in the successive dishes. When it came to the black coffee, and then to the 'petits verres' of cognac, with lumps of sugar set fire to atop, it was something that so far transcended my home-kept experience that it began to seem altogether visionary.

Neither Fields nor Doctor Holmes smoked, and I had to confess that I did not; but Lowell smoked enough for all three, and the spark of his cigar began to show in the waning light before we rose from the table. The time that never had, nor can ever have, its fellow for me, had to come to an end, as all times must, and when I shook hands with Lowell in parting, he overwhelmed me by saying that if I thought of going to Concord he would send me a letter to Hawthorne. I was not to see Lowell again during my stay in Boston; but Doctor Holmes asked me to tea for the next evening, and Fields said I must come to breakfast with him in the morning.

XI.

I recall with the affection due to his friendly nature, and to the kindness afterwards to pass between us for many years, the whole aspect of the publisher when I first saw him. His abundant hair, and his full "beard as broad as ony spade," that flowed from his throat in Homeric curls, were touched with the first frost. He had a fine color, and his eyes, as keen as they were kind, twinkled restlessly above the wholesome russet-red of his cheeks. His portly frame was clad in those Scotch tweeds which had not yet displaced the traditional broadcloth with us in the West, though I had sent to New York for a rough suit, and so felt myself not quite unworthy to meet a man fresh from the hands of the London tailor.

Otherwise I stood as much in awe of him as his jovial soul would let me; and if I might I should like to suggest to the literary youth of this day some notion of the importance of his name to the literary youth of my day. He gave aesthetic character to the house of Ticknor & Fields, but he was by no means a silent partner on the economic side. No one can forecast the fortune of a new book, but he knew as well as any publisher can know not only whether a book was good, but whether the reader would think so; and I suppose that his house made as few bad guesses, along with their good ones, as any house that ever tried the uncertain temper of the public with its ventures. In the minds of all who loved the plain brown cloth and tasteful print of its issues he was more or less intimately associated with their literature; and those who were not mistaken in thinking De Quincey one of the delightfulest authors in the world, were especially grateful to the man who first edited his writings in book form, and proud that this edition was the effect of American sympathy with them. At that day, I believed authorship the noblest calling in the world, and I should still be at a loss to name any nobler. The great authors I had met were to me the sum of greatness, and if I could not rank their publisher with them by virtue of equal achievement, I handsomely brevetted him worthy of their friendship, and honored him in the visible measure of it.

In his house beside the Charles, and in the close neighborhood of Doctor Holmes, I found an odor and an air of books such as I fancied might belong to the famous literary houses of London. It is still there, that friendly home of lettered refinement, and the gracious spirit which knew how to welcome me, and make the least of my shyness and strangeness, and the most of the little else there was in me, illumines it still, though my host of that rapturous moment has many years been of those who are only with us unseen and unheard. I remember his burlesque pretence that morning of an inextinguishable grief when I owned that I had never eaten blueberry cake before, and how he kept returning to the pathos of the fact that there should be a region of the earth where blueberry cake was unknown. We breakfasted in the pretty room whose windows look out through leaves and flowers upon the river's coming and going tides, and whose walls were covered with the faces and the autographs of all the contemporary poets and novelists. The Fieldses had spent some days with Tennyson in their recent English sojourn, and Mrs. Fields had much to tell of him, how he looked, how he smoked, how he read aloud, and how he said, when he asked her to go with him to the tower of his house, "Come up and see the sad English sunset!" which had an instant value to me such as some rich verse of his might have had. I was very new to it all, how new I could not very well say, but I flattered myself that I breathed in that atmosphere as if in the return from life-long exile. Still I patriotically bragged of the West a little, and I told them proudly that in Columbus no book since Uncle Tom's Cabin had sold so well as 'The Marble Faun'. This made the effect that I wished, but whether it was true or not, Heaven knows; I only know that I heard it from our leading bookseller, and I made no question of it myself.

After breakfast, Fields went away to the office, and I lingered, while Mrs. Fields showed me from shelf to shelf in the library, and dazzled me with the sight of authors' copies, and volumes invaluable with the autographs and the pencilled notes of the men whose names were dear to me from my love of their work. Everywhere was some souvenir of the living celebrities my hosts had met; and whom had they not met in that English sojourn in days before England embittered herself to us during our civil war? Not Tennyson only, but Thackeray, but Dickens, but Charles Reade, but Carlyle, but many a minor fame was in my ears from converse so recent with them that it was as if I heard their voices in their echoed words.

I do not remember how long I stayed; I remember I was afraid of staying too long, and so I am sure I did not stay as long as I should have liked. But I have not the least notion how I got away, and I am not certain where I spent the rest of a day that began in the clouds, but had to be ended on the common earth. I suppose I gave it mostly to wandering about the city, and partly to recording my impressions of it for that newspaper which never published them. The summer weather in Boston, with its sunny heat struck through and through with the coolness of the sea, and its clear air untainted with a breath of smoke, I have always loved, but it had then a zest unknown before; and I should have thought it enough simply to be alive in it. But everywhere I came upon something that fed my famine for the old, the quaint, the picturesque, and however the day passed it was a banquet, a festival. I can only recall my breathless first sight of the Public Library and of the Athenaeum Gallery: great sights then, which the Vatican and the Pitti hardly afterwards eclipsed for mere emotion. In fact I did not see these elder treasuries of literature and art between breakfasting with the Autocrat's publisher in the morning, and taking tea with the Autocrat himself in the evening, and that made a whole world's difference.

XII.

The tea of that simpler time is wholly inconceivable to this generation, which knows the thing only as a mild form of afternoon reception; but I suppose that in 1860 very few dined late in our whole pastoral republic. Tea was the meal people asked people to when they wished to sit at long leisure and large ease; it came at the end of the day, at six o'clock, or seven; and one went to it in morning dress. It had an unceremonied domesticity in the abundance of its light dishes, and I fancy these did not vary much from East to West, except that we had a Southern touch in our fried chicken and corn bread; but at the Autocrat's tea table the cheering cup had a flavor unknown to me before that day. He asked me if I knew it, and I said it was English breakfast tea; for I had drunk it at the publisher's in the morning, and was willing not to seem strange to it. "Ah, yes," he said; "but this is the flower of the souchong; it is the blossom, the poetry of tea," and then he told me how it had been given him by a friend, a merchant in the China trade, which used to flourish in Boston, and was the poetry of commerce, as this delicate beverage was of tea. That commerce is long past, and I fancy that the plant ceased to bloom when the traffic fell into decay.

The Autocrat's windows had the same outlook upon the Charles as the publisher's, and after tea we went up into a back parlor of the same orientation, and saw the sunset die over the water, and the westering flats and hills. Nowhere else in the world has the day a lovelier close, and our talk took something of the mystic coloring that the heavens gave those mantling expanses. It was chiefly his talk, but I have always found the best talkers are willing that you should talk if you like, and a quick sympathy and a subtle sense met all that I had to say from him and from the unbroken circle of kindred intelligences about him. I saw him then in the midst of his family, and perhaps never afterwards to better advantage, or in a finer mood. We spoke of the things that people perhaps once liked to deal with more than they do now; of the intimations of immortality, of the experiences of morbid youth, and of all those messages from the tremulous nerves which we take for prophecies. I was not ashamed, before his tolerant wisdom, to acknowledge the effects that had lingered so long with me in fancy and even in conduct, from a time of broken health and troubled spirit; and I remember the exquisite tact in him which recognized them as things common to all, however peculiar in each, which left them mine for whatever obscure vanity I might have in them, and yet gave me the companionship of the whole race in their experience. We spoke of forebodings and presentiments; we approached the mystic confines of the world from which no traveller has yet returned with a passport 'en regle' and properly 'vise'; and he held his light course through these filmy impalpabilities with a charming sincerity, with the scientific conscience that refuses either to deny the substance of things unseen, or to affirm it. In the gathering dusk, so weird did my fortune of being there and listening to him seem, that I might well have been a blessed ghost, for all the reality I felt in myself.

I tried to tell him how much I had read him from my boyhood, and with what joy and gain; and he was patient of these futilities, and I have no doubt imagined the love that inspired them, and accepted that instead of the poor praise. When the sunset passed, and the lamps were lighted, and we all came back to our dear little firmset earth, he began to question me about my native region of it. From many forgotten inquiries I recall his asking me what was the fashionable religion in Columbus, or the Church that socially corresponded to the Unitarian Church in Boston. He had first to clarify my intelligence as to what Unitarianism was; we had Universalists but not Unitarians; but when I understood, I answered from such vantage as my own wholly outside Swedenborgianism gave me, that I thought most of the most respectable people with us were of the Presbyterian Church; some were certainly Episcopalians, but upon the whole the largest number were Presbyterians. He found that very strange indeed; and said that he did not believe there was a Presbyterian Church in Boston; that the New England Calvinists were all of the Orthodox Church. He had to explain Oxthodoxy to me, and then I could confess to one Congregational Church in Columbus.

Probably I failed to give the Autocrat any very clear image of our social frame in the West, but the fault was altogether mine, if I did.

Such lecturing tours as he had made had not taken him among us, as those of Emerson and other New-Englanders had, and my report was positive rather than comparative. I was full of pride in journalism at that day, and I dare say that I vaunted the brilliancy and power of our newspapers more than they merited; I should not have been likely to wrong them otherwise. It is strange that in all the talk I had with him and Lowell, or rather heard from them, I can recall nothing said of political affairs, though Lincoln had then been nominated by the Republicans, and the Civil War had practically begun. But we did not imagine such a thing in the North; we rested secure in the belief that if Lincoln were elected the South would eat all its fiery words, perhaps from the mere love and inveterate habit of fire-eating.

I rent myself away from the Autocrat's presence as early as I could, and as my evening had been too full of happiness to sleep upon at once, I spent the rest of the night till two in the morning wandering about the streets and in the Common with a Harvard Senior whom I had met. He was a youth of like literary passions with myself, but of such different traditions in every possible way that his deeply schooled and definitely regulated life seemed as anomalous to me as my own desultory and self-found way must have seemed to him. We passed the time in the delight of trying to make ourselves known to each other, and in a promise to continue by letter the effort, which duly lapsed into silent patience with the necessarily insoluble problem.

XIII.

I must have lingered in Boston for the introduction to Hawthorne which Lowell had offered me, for when it came, with a little note of kindness and counsel for myself such as only Lowell had the gift of writing, it was already so near Sunday that I stayed over till Monday before I started. I do not recall what I did with the time, except keep myself from making it a burden to the people I knew, and wandering about the city alone. Nothing of it remains to me except the fortune that favored me that Sunday night with a view of the old Granary Burying-ground on Tremont Street. I found the gates open, and I explored every path in the place, wreaking myself in such meagre emotion as I could get from the tomb of the Franklin family, and rejoicing with the whole soul of my Western modernity in the evidence of a remote antiquity which so many of the dim inscriptions afforded. I do not think that I have ever known anything practically older than these monuments, though I have since supped so full of classic and mediaeval ruin. I am sure that I was more deeply touched by the epitaph of a poor little Puritan maiden who died at sixteen in the early sixteen-thirties than afterwards by the tomb of Caecilia Metella, and that the heartache which I tried to put into verse when I got back to my room in the hotel was none the less genuine because it would not lend itself to my literary purpose, and remains nothing but pathos to this day.

I am not able to say how I reached the town of Lowell, where I went before going to Concord, that I might ease the unhappy conscience I had about those factories which I hated so much to see, and have it clean for the pleasure of meeting the fabricator of visions whom I was authorized to molest in any air-castle where I might find him. I only know that I went to Lowell, and visited one of the great mills, which with their whirring spools, the ceaseless flight of their shuttles, and the bewildering sight and sound of all their mechanism have since seemed to me the death of the joy that ought to come from work, if not the captivity of those who tended them. But then I thought it right and well for me to be standing by,

"With sick and scornful looks averse,"

while these others toiled; I did not see the tragedy in it, and I got my pitiful literary antipathy away as soon as I could, no wiser for the sight of the ingenious contrivances I inspected, and I am sorry to say no sadder. In the cool of the evening I sat at the door of my hotel, and watched the long files of the work-worn factory-girls stream by, with no concern for them but to see which was pretty and which was plain, and with no dream of a truer order than that which gave them ten hours' work a day in those hideous mills and lodged them in the barracks where they rested from their toil.

I wonder if there is a stage that still runs between Lowell and Concord, past meadow walls, and under the caressing boughs of way-side elms, and through the bird-haunted gloom of woodland roads, in the freshness of the summer morning? By a blessed chance I found that there was such a stage in 1860, and I took it from my hotel, instead of going back to Boston and up to Concord as I must have had to do by train. The journey gave me the intimacy of the New England country as I could have had it in no other fashion, and for the first time I saw it in all the summer sweetness which I have often steeped my soul in since. The meadows were newly mown, and the air was fragrant with the grass, stretching in long winrows among the brown bowlders, or capped with canvas in the little haycocks it had been gathered into the day before. I was fresh from the affluent farms of the Western Reserve, and this care of the grass touched me with a rude pity, which I also bestowed on the meagre fields of corn and wheat; but still the land was lovelier than any I had ever seen, with its old farmhouses, and brambled gray stone walls, its stony hillsides, its staggering orchards, its wooded tops, and its thick-brackened valleys. From West to East the difference was as great as I afterwards found it from America to Europe, and my impression of something quaint and strange was no keener when I saw Old England the next year than when I saw New England now. I had imagined the landscape bare of trees, and I was astonished to find it almost as full of them as at home, though they all looked very little, as they well might to eyes used to the primeval forests of Ohio. The road ran through them from time to time, and took their coolness on its smooth hard reaches, and then issued again in the glisten of the open fields.

I made phrases to myself about the scenery as we drove along; and yes, I suppose I made phrases about the young girl who was one of the inside passengers, and who, when the common strangeness had somewhat worn off, began to sing, and sang most of the way to Concord. Perhaps she was not very sage, and I am sure she was not of the caste of Vere de Vere, but she was pretty enough, and she had a voice of a bird-like tunableness, so that I would not have her out of the memory of that pleasant journey if I could. She was long ago an elderly woman, if she lives, and I suppose she would not now point out her fellow-passenger if he strolled in the evening by the house where she had dismounted, upon her arrival in Concord, and laugh and pull another girl away from the window, in the high excitement of the prodigious adventure.

XV.

Her fellow-passenger was in far other excitement; he was to see Hawthorne, and in a manner to meet Priscilla and Zenobia, and Hester Prynne and little Pearl, and Miriam and Hilda, and Hollingsworth and Coverdale, and Chillingworth and Dimmesdale, and Donatello and Kenyon; and he had no heart for any such poor little reality as that, who could not have been got into any story that one could respect, and must have been difficult even in a Heinesque poem.

I wasted that whole evening and the next morning in fond delaying, and it was not until after the indifferent dinner I got at the tavern where I stopped, that I found courage to go and present Lowell's letter to Hawthorne. I would almost have foregone meeting the weird genius only to have kept that letter, for it said certain infinitely precious things of me with such a sweetness, such a grace, as Lowell alone could give his praise. Years afterwards, when Hawthorne was dead, I met Mrs. Hawthorne, and told her of the pang I had in parting with it, and she sent it me, doubly enriched by Hawthorne's keeping. But now if I were to see him at all I must give up my letter, and I carried it in my hand to the door of the cottage he called The Wayside. It was never otherwise than a very modest place, but the modesty was greater then than to-day, and there was already some preliminary carpentry at one end of the cottage, which I saw was to result in an addition to it. I recall pleasant fields across the road before it; behind rose a hill wooded with low pines, such as is made in Septimius Felton the scene of the involuntary duel between Septimius and the young British officer. I have a sense of the woods coming quite down to the house, but if this was so I do not know what to do with a grassy slope which seems to have stretched part way up the hill. As I approached, I looked for the tower which the author was fabled to climb into at sight of the coming guest, and pull the ladder up after him; and I wondered whether he would fly before me in that sort, or imagine some easier means of escaping me.

The door was opened to my ring by a tall handsome boy whom I suppose to have been Mr. Julian Hawthorne; and the next moment I found myself in the presence of the romancer, who entered from some room beyond. He advanced carrying his head with a heavy forward droop, and with a pace for which I decided that the word would be pondering. It was the pace of a bulky man of fifty, and his head was that beautiful head we all know from the many pictures of it. But Hawthorne's look was different from that of any picture of him that I have seen. It was sombre and brooding, as the look of such a poet should have been; it was the look of a man who had dealt faithfully and therefore sorrowfully with that problem of evil which forever attracted, forever evaded Hawthorne. It was by no means troubled; it was full of a dark repose. Others who knew him better and saw him oftener were familiar with other aspects, and I remember that one night at Longfellow's table, when one of the guests happened to speak of the photograph of Hawthorne which hung in a corner of the room, Lowell said, after a glance at it, "Yes, it's good; but it hasn't his fine 'accipitral' [pertaining to the look of a bird of prey; hawklike. D.W.] look."

In the face that confronted me, however, there was nothing of keen alertness; but only a sort of quiet, patient intelligence, for which I seek the right word in vain. It was a very regular face, with beautiful eyes; the mustache, still entirely dark, was dense over the fine mouth. Hawthorne was dressed in black, and he had a certain effect which I remember, of seeming to have on a black cravat with no visible collar. He was such a man that if I had ignorantly met him anywhere I should have instantly felt him to be a personage.

I must have given him the letter myself, for I have no recollection of parting with it before, but I only remember his offering me his hand, and making me shyly and tentatively welcome. After a few moments of the demoralization which followed his hospitable attempts in me, he asked if I would not like to go up on his hill with him and sit there, where he smoked in the afternoon. He offered me a cigar, and when I said that I did not smoke, he lighted it for himself, and we climbed the hill together. At the top, where there was an outlook in the pines over the Concord meadows, we found a log, and he invited me to a place on it beside him, and at intervals of a minute or so he talked while he smoked. Heaven preserved me from the folly of trying to tell him how much his books had been to me, and though we got on rapidly at no time, I think we got on better for this interposition. He asked me about Lowell, I dare say, for I told him of my joy in meeting him and Doctor Holmes, and this seemed greatly to interest him. Perhaps because he was so lately from Europe, where our great men are always seen through the wrong end of the telescope, he appeared surprised at my devotion, and asked me whether I cared as much for meeting them as I should care for meeting the famous English authors. I professed that I cared much more, though whether this was true, I now have my doubts, and I think Hawthorne doubted it at the time. But he said nothing in comment, and went on to speak generally of Europe and America. He was curious about the West, which he seemed to fancy much more purely American, and said he would like to see some part of the country on which the shadow (or, if I must be precise, the damned shadow) of Europe had not fallen. I told him I thought the West must finally be characterized by the Germans, whom we had in great numbers, and, purely from my zeal for German poetry, I tried to allege some proofs of their present influence, though I could think of none outside of politics, which I thought they affected wholesomely. I knew Hawthorne was a Democrat, and I felt it well to touch politics lightly, but he had no more to say about the fateful election then pending than Holmes or Lowell had.

With the abrupt transition of his talk throughout, he began somehow to speak of women, and said he had never seen a woman whom he thought quite beautiful. In the same way he spoke of the New England temperament, and suggested that the apparent coldness in it was also real, and that the suppression of emotion for generations would extinguish it at last. Then he questioned me as to my knowledge of Concord, and whether I had seen any of the notable people. I answered that I had met no one but himself, as yet, but I very much wished to see Emerson and Thoreau. I did not think it needful to say that I wished to see Thoreau quite as much because he had suffered in the cause of John Brown as because he had written the books which had taken me; and when he said that Thoreau prided himself on coming nearer the heart of a pine-tree than any other human being, I could say honestly enough that I would rather come near the heart of a man. This visibly pleased him, and I saw that it did not displease him, when he asked whether I was not going to see his next neighbor, Mr. Alcott, and I confessed that I had never heard of him. That surprised as well as pleased him; he remarked, with whatever intention, that there was nothing like recognition to make a man modest; and he entered into some account of the philosopher, whom I suppose I need not be much ashamed of not knowing then, since his influence was of the immediate sort that makes a man important to his townsmen while he is still strange to his countrymen.

Hawthorne descanted a little upon the landscape, and said certain of the pleasant fields below us be longed to him; but he preferred his hill-top, and if he could have his way those arable fields should be grown up to pines too. He smoked fitfully, and slowly, and in the hour that we spent together, his whiffs were of the desultory and unfinal character of his words. When we went down, he asked me into his house again, and would have me stay to tea, for which we found the table laid. But there was a great deal of silence in it all, and at times, in spite of his shadowy kindness, I felt my spirits sink. After tea, he showed me a book case, where there were a few books toppling about on the half-filled shelves, and said, coldly, "This is my library." I knew that men were his books, and though I myself cared for books so much, I found it fit and fine that he should care so little, or seem to care so little. Some of his own romances were among the volumes on these shelves, and when I put my finger on the 'Blithedale Romance' and said that I preferred that to the others, his face lighted up, and he said that he believed the Germans liked that best too.

Upon the whole we parted such good friends that when I offered to take leave he asked me how long I was to be in Concord, and not only bade me come to see him again, but said he would give me a card to Emerson, if I liked. I answered, of course, that I should like it beyond all things; and he wrote on the back of his card something which I found, when I got away, to be, "I find this young man worthy." The quaintness, the little stiffness of it, if one pleases to call it so, was amusing to one who was not without his sense of humor, but the kindness filled me to the throat with joy. In fact, I entirely liked Hawthorne. He had been as cordial as so shy a man could show himself; and I perceived, with the repose that nothing else can give, the entire sincerity of his soul.

Nothing could have been further from the behavior of this very great man than any sort of posing, apparently, or a wish to affect me with a sense of his greatness. I saw that he was as much abashed by our encounter as I was; he was visibly shy to the point of discomfort, but in no ignoble sense was he conscious, and as nearly as he could with one so much his younger he made an absolute equality between us. My memory of him is without alloy one of the finest pleasures of my life: In my heart I paid him the same glad homage that I paid Lowell and Holmes, and he did nothing to make me think that I had overpaid him. This seems perhaps very little to say in his praise, but to my mind it is saying everything, for I have known but few great men, especially of those I met in early life, when I wished to lavish my admiration upon them, whom I have not the impression of having left in my debt. Then, a defect of the Puritan quality, which I have found in many New-Englanders, is that, wittingly or unwittingly, they propose themselves to you as an example, or if not quite this, that they surround themselves with a subtle ether of potential disapprobation, in which, at the first sign of unworthiness in you, they helplessly suffer you to gasp and perish; they have good hearts, and they would probably come to your succor out of humanity, if they knew how, but they do not know how. Hawthorne had nothing of this about him; he was no more tacitly than he was explicitly didactic. I thought him as thoroughly in keeping with his romances as Doctor Holmes had seemed with his essays and poems, and I met him as I had met the Autocrat in the supreme hour of his fame. He had just given the world the last of those incomparable works which it was to have finished from his hand; the 'Marble Faun' had worthily followed, at a somewhat longer interval than usual, the 'Blithedale Romance', and the 'House of Seven Gables', and the 'Scarlet Letter', and had, perhaps carried his name higher than all the rest, and certainly farther. Everybody was reading it, and more or less bewailing its indefinite close, but yielding him that full honor and praise which a writer can hope for but once in his life. Nobody dreamed that thereafter only precious fragments, sketches more or less faltering, though all with the divine touch in them, were further to enrich a legacy which in its kind is the finest the race has received from any mind. As I have said, we are always finding new Hawthornes, but the illusion soon wears away, and then we perceive that they were not Hawthornes at all; that he had some peculiar difference from them, which, by and-by, we shall no doubt consent must be his difference from all men evermore.

I am painfully aware that I have not summoned before the reader the image of the man as it has always stood in my memory, and I feel a sort of shame for my failure. He was so altogether simple that it seems as if it would be easy to do so; but perhaps a spirit from the other world would be simple too, and yet would no more stand at parle, or consent to be sketched, than Hawthorne. In fact, he was always more or less merging into the shadow, which was in a few years wholly to close over him; there was nothing uncanny in his presence, there was nothing even unwilling, but he had that apparitional quality of some great minds which kept Shakespeare largely unknown to those who thought themselves his intimates, and has at last left him a sort of doubt. There was nothing teasing or wilfully elusive in Hawthorne's impalpability, such as I afterwards felt in Thoreau; if he was not there to your touch, it was no fault of his; it was because your touch was dull, and wanted the use of contact with such natures. The hand passes through the veridical phantom without a sense of its presence, but the phantom is none the less veridical for all that.

XVI.

I kept the evening of the day I met Hawthorne wholly for the thoughts of him, or rather for that reverberation which continues in the young sensibilities after some important encounter. It must have been the next morning that I went to find Thoreau, and I am dimly aware of making one or two failures to find him, if I ever really found him at all.

He is an author who has fallen into that abeyance, awaiting all authors, great or small, at some time or another; but I think that with him, at least in regard to his most important book, it can be only transitory. I have not read the story of his hermitage beside Walden Pond since the year 1858, but I have a fancy that if I should take it up now, I should think it a wiser and truer conception of the world than I thought it then. It is no solution of the problem; men are not going to answer the riddle of the painful earth by building themselves shanties and living upon beans and watching ant-fights; but I do not believe Tolstoy himself has more clearly shown the hollowness, the hopelessness, the unworthiness of the life of the world than Thoreau did in that book. If it were newly written it could not fail of a far vaster acceptance than it had then, when to those who thought and felt seriously it seemed that if slavery could only be controlled, all things else would come right of themselves with us. Slavery has not only been controlled, but it has been destroyed, and yet things have not begun to come right with us; but it was in the order of Providence that chattel slavery should cease before industrial slavery, and the infinitely crueler and stupider vanity and luxury bred of it, should be attacked. If there was then any prevision of the struggle now at hand, the seers averted their eyes, and strove only to cope with the less evil. Thoreau himself, who had so clear a vision of the falsity and folly of society as we still have it, threw himself into the tide that was already, in Kansas and Virginia, reddened with war; he aided and abetted the John Brown raid, I do not recall how much or in what sort; and he had suffered in prison for his opinions and actions. It was this inevitable heroism of his that, more than his literature even, made me wish to see him and revere him; and I do not believe that I should have found the veneration difficult, when at last I met him in his insufficient person, if he had otherwise been present to my glowing expectation. He came into the room a quaint, stump figure of a man, whose effect of long trunk and short limbs was heightened by his fashionless trousers being let down too low. He had a noble face, with tossed hair, a distraught eye, and a fine aquilinity of profile, which made me think at once of Don Quixote and of Cervantes; but his nose failed to add that foot to his stature which Lamb says a nose of that shape will always give a man. He tried to place me geographically after he had given me a chair not quite so far off as Ohio, though still across the whole room, for he sat against one wall, and I against the other; but apparently he failed to pull himself out of his revery by the effort, for he remained in a dreamy muse, which all my attempts to say something fit about John Brown and Walden Pond seemed only to deepen upon him. I have not the least doubt that I was needless and valueless about both, and that what I said could not well have prompted an important response; but I did my poor best, and I was terribly disappointed in the result. The truth is that in those days I was a helplessly concrete young person, and all forms of the abstract, the air-drawn, afflicted me like physical discomforts. I do not remember that Thoreau spoke of his books or of himself at all, and when he began to speak of John Brown, it was not the warm, palpable, loving, fearful old man of my conception, but a sort of John Brown type, a John Brown ideal, a John Brown principle, which we were somehow (with long pauses between the vague, orphic phrases) to cherish, and to nourish ourselves upon.

It was not merely a defeat of my hopes, it was a rout, and I felt myself so scattered over the field of thought that I could hardly bring my forces together for retreat. I must have made some effort, vain and foolish enough, to rematerialize my old demigod, but when I came away it was with the feeling that there was very little more left of John Brown than there was of me. His body was not mouldering in the grave, neither was his soul marching on; his ideal, his type, his principle alone existed, and I did not know what to do with it. I am not blaming Thoreau; his words were addressed to a far other understanding than mine, and it was my misfortune if I could not profit by them. I think, or I venture to hope, that I could profit better by them now; but in this record I am trying honestly to report their effect with the sort of youth I was then.

XVII.

Such as I was, I rather wonder that I had the courage, after this experiment of Thoreau, to present the card Hawthorne had given me to Emerson. I must have gone to him at once, however, for I cannot make out any interval of time between my visit to the disciple and my visit to the master. I think it was Emerson himself who opened his door to me, for I have a vision of the fine old man standing tall on his threshold, with the card in his hand, and looking from it to me with a vague serenity, while I waited a moment on the door-step below him. He must then have been about sixty, but I remember nothing of age in his aspect, though I have called him an old man. His hair, I am sure, was still entirely dark, and his face had a kind of marble youthfulness, chiselled to a delicate intelligence by the highest and noblest thinking that any man has done. There was a strange charm in Emerson's eyes, which I felt then and always, something like that I saw in Lincoln's, but shyer, but sweeter and less sad. His smile was the very sweetest I have ever beheld, and the contour of the mask and the line of the profile were in keeping with this incomparable sweetness of the mouth, at once grave and quaint, though quaint is not quite the word for it either, but subtly, not unkindly arch, which again is not the word.

It was his great fortune to have been mostly misunderstood, and to have reached the dense intelligence of his fellow-men after a whole lifetime of perfectly simple and lucid appeal, and his countenance expressed the patience and forbearance of a wise man content to bide his time. It would be hard to persuade people now that Emerson once represented to the popular mind all that was most hopelessly impossible, and that in a certain sort he was a national joke, the type of the incomprehensible, the byword of the poor paragrapher. He had perhaps disabused the community somewhat by presenting himself here and there as a lecturer, and talking face to face with men in terms which they could not refuse to find as clear as they were wise; he was more and more read, by certain persons, here and there; but we are still so far behind him in the reach of his far-thinking that it need not be matter of wonder that twenty years before his death he was the most misunderstood man in America. Yet in that twilight where he dwelt he loomed large upon the imagination; the minds that could not conceive him were still aware of his greatness. I myself had not read much of him, but I knew the essays he was printing in the Atlantic, and I knew certain of his poems, though by no means many; yet I had this sense of him, that he was somehow, beyond and above my ken, a presence of force and beauty and wisdom, uncompanioned in our literature. He had lately stooped from his ethereal heights to take part in the battle of humanity, and I suppose that if the truth were told he was more to my young fervor because he had said that John Brown had made the gallows glorious like the cross, than because he had uttered all those truer and wiser things which will still a hundred years hence be leading the thought of the world.

I do not know in just what sort he made me welcome, but I am aware of sitting with him in his study or library, and of his presently speaking of Hawthorne, whom I probably celebrated as I best could, and whom he praised for his personal excellence, and for his fine qualities as a neighbor. "But his last book," he added, reflectively, "is a mere mush," and I perceived that this great man was no better equipped to judge an artistic fiction than the groundlings who were then crying out upon the indefinite close of the Marble Faun. Apparently he had read it, as they had, for the story, but it seems to me now, if it did not seem to me then, that as far as the problem of evil was involved, the book must leave it where it found it. That is forever insoluble, and it was rather with that than with his more or less shadowy people that the romancer was concerned. Emerson had, in fact, a defective sense as to specific pieces of literature; he praised extravagantly, and in the wrong place, especially among the new things, and he failed to see the worth of much that was fine and precious beside the line of his fancy.

He began to ask me about the West, and about some unknown man in Michigan; who had been sending him poems, and whom he seemed to think very promising, though he has not apparently kept his word to do great things. I did not find what Emerson had to say of my section very accurate or important, though it was kindly enough, and just enough as to what the West ought to do in litera-

But I had not the courage to speak of the affair to any one but Fields, to whom I unpacked my heart when I got back to Boston, and he asked me about my adventures in Concord. By this time I could see it in a humorous light, and I did not much mind his lying back in his chair and laughing and laughing, till I thought he would roll out of it. He perfectly conceived the situation, and got an amusement from it that I could get only through sympathy with him. But I thought it a favorable moment to propose myself as the assistant editor of the Atlantic Monthly, which I had the belief I could very well become, with advantage to myself if not to the magazine. He seemed to think so too; he said that if the place had not just been filled, I should certainly have had it; and it was to his recollection of this prompt ambition of mine that I suppose I may have owed my succession to a like vacancy some four years later. He was charmingly kind; he entered with the sweetest interest into the story of my economic life, which had been full of changes and chances already. But when I said very seriously that now I was tired of these fortuities, and would like to be settled in something, he asked, with dancing eyes,

"Why, how old are you?"

"I am twenty-three," I answered, and then the laughing fit took him again.

"Well," he said, "you begin young, out there!"

In my heart I did not think that twenty-three was so very young, but perhaps it was; and if any one were to say that I had been portraying here a youth whose aims were certainly beyond his achievements, who was morbidly sensitive, and if not conceited was intolerably conscious, who had met with incredible kindness, and had suffered no more than was good for him, though he might not have merited his pain any more than his joy, I do not know that I should gainsay him, for I am not at all sure that I was not just that kind of youth when I paid my first visit to New England.

LITERARY FRIENDS AND ACQUAINTANCES—First Impressions
of Literary New
York

by William Dean Howells

FIRST IMPRESSIONS OF LITERARY NEW YORK

It was by boat that I arrived from Boston, on an August morning
of 1860, which was probably of the same quality as an August
morning of 1900. I used not to mind the weather much in those
days; it was hot or it was cold, it was wet or it was dry, but it was
not my affair; and I suppose that I sweltered about the strange city,
with no sense of anything very personal in the temperature, until
nightfall. What I remember is being high up in a hotel long since
laid low, listening in the summer dark, after the long day was done,
to the Niagara roar of the omnibuses whose tide then swept Broadway from curb to curb, for all the miles of its length. At that hour
the other city noises were stilled, or lost in this vaster volume of
sound, which seemed to fill the whole night. It had a solemnity
which the modern comer to New York will hardly imagine, for that
tide of omnibuses has long since ebbed away, and has left the air to
the strident discords of the elevated trains and the irregular alarum
of the grip-car gongs, which blend to no such harmonious thunder
as rose from the procession of those ponderous and innumerable
vans. There was a sort of inner quiet in the sound, and when I chose
I slept off to it, and woke to it in the morning refreshed and
strengthened to explore the literary situation in the metropolis.

I.

Not that I think I left this to the second day. Very probably I lost no time in going to the office of the Saturday Press, as soon as I had my breakfast after arriving, and I have a dim impression of anticipating the earliest of the Bohemians, whose gay theory of life obliged them to a good many hardships in lying down early in the morning, and rising up late in the day. If it was the office-boy who bore me company during the first hour of my visit, by-and-by the editors and contributors actually began to come in. I would not be very specific about them if I could, for since that Bohemia has faded from the map of the republic of letters, it has grown more and more difficult to trace its citizenship to any certain writer. There are some living who knew the Bohemians and even loved them, but there are increasingly few who were of them, even in the fond retrospect of youthful follies and errors. It was in fact but a sickly colony, transplanted from the mother asphalt of Paris, and never really striking root in the pavements of New York; it was a colony of ideas, of theories, which had perhaps never had any deep root anywhere. What these ideas, these theories, were in art and in life, it would not be very easy to say; but in the Saturday Press they came to violent expression, not to say explosion, against all existing forms of respectability. If respectability was your 'bete noire', then you were a Bohemian; and if you were in the habit of rendering yourself in prose, then you necessarily shredded your prose into very fine paragraphs of a sentence each, or of a very few words, or even of one word. I believe this fashion prevailed till very lately with some of the dramatic critics, who thought that it gave a quality of epigram to the style; and I suppose it was borrowed from the more spasmodic moments of Victor Hugo by the editor of the Press. He brought it back with him when he came home from one of those sojourns in Paris which possess one of the French accent rather than the French language; I long desired to write in that fashion myself, but I had not the courage.

This editor was a man of such open and avowed cynicism that he may have been, for all I know, a kindly optimist at heart; some say, however, that he had really talked himself into being what he seemed. I only know that his talk, the first day I saw him, was of such a sort that if he was half as bad, he would have been too bad to be. He walked up and down his room saying what lurid things he would directly do if any one accused him of respectability, so that he might disabuse the minds of all witnesses. There were four or five of his assistants and contributors listening to the dreadful threats, which did not deceive even so great innocence as mine, but I do not know whether they found it the sorry farce that I did. They probably felt the fascination for him which I could not disown, in spite of my inner disgust; and were watchful at the same time for the effect of his words with one who was confessedly fresh from Boston, and was full of delight in the people he had seen there. It appeared, with him, to be proof of the inferiority of Boston that if you passed down Washington Street, half a dozen men in the crowd would know you were Holmes, or Lowell, or Longfellow, or Wendell Phillips; but in Broadway no one would know who you were, or care to the measure of his smallest blasphemy. I have since heard this more than once urged as a signal advantage of New York for the aesthetic inhabitant, but I am not sure, yet, that it is so. The unrecognized celebrity probably has his mind quite as much upon himself as if some one pointed him out, and otherwise I cannot think that the sense of neighborhood is such a bad thing for the artist in any sort. It involves the sense of responsibility, which cannot be too constant or too keen. If it narrows, it deepens; and this may be the secret of Boston.

It would not be easy to say just why the Bohemian group represented New York literature to my imagination; for I certainly associated other names with its best work, but perhaps it was because I had written for the Saturday Press myself, and had my pride in it, and perhaps it was because that paper really embodied the new literary life of the city. It was clever, and full of the wit that tries its teeth upon everything. It attacked all literary shams but its own, and it made itself felt and feared. The young writers throughout the country were ambitious to be seen in it, and they gave their best to it; they gave literally, for the Saturday Press never paid in anything but hopes of paying, vaguer even than promises. It is not too much to say that it was very nearly as well for one to be accepted by the Press as to be accepted by the Atlantic, and for the time there was no other literary comparison. To be in it was to be in the company of Fitz James O'Brien, Fitzhugh Ludlow, Mr. Aldrich, Mr. Stedman, and whoever else was liveliest in prose or loveliest in verse at that day in New York. It was a power, and although it is true that, as Henry Giles said of it, "Man cannot live by snapping-turtle alone," the Press was very good snapping-turtle. Or, it seemed so then; I should be almost afraid to test it now, for I do not like snapping-turtle so much as I once did, and I have grown nicer in my taste, and want my snapping-turtle of the very best. What is certain is that I went to the office of the Saturday Press in New York with much the same sort of feeling I had in going to the office of the Atlantic Monthly in Boston, but I came away with a very different feeling. I had found there a bitterness against Boston as great as the bitterness against respectability, and as Boston was then rapidly becoming my second country, I could not join in the scorn thought of her and said of her by the Bohemians. I fancied a conspiracy among them to shock the literary pilgrim, and to minify the precious emotions he had experienced in visiting other shrines; but I found no harm in that, for I knew just how much to be shocked, and I thought I knew better how to value certain things of the soul than they. Yet when their chief asked me how I got on with Hawthorne, and I began to say that he was very shy and I was rather shy, and the king of Bohemia took his pipe out to break in upon me with "Oh, a couple of shysters!" and the rest laughed, I was abashed all they could have wished, and was not restored to myself till one of them said that the thought of Boston made him as ugly as sin; then I began to hope again that men who took themselves so seriously as that need not be taken very seriously by me.

In fact I had heard things almost as desperately cynical in other newspaper offices before that, and I could not see what was so distinctively Bohemian in these 'anime prave', these souls so baleful by their own showing. But apparently Bohemia was not a state that you could well imagine from one encounter, and since my stay in New York was to be very short, I lost no time in acquainting myself further with it. That very night I went to the beer-cellar, once very far up Broadway, where I was given to know that the Bohemian nights were smoked and quaffed away. It was said, so far West as Ohio, that the queen of Bohemia sometimes came to Pfaff's: a young girl of a sprightly gift in letters, whose name or pseudonym had made itself pretty well known at that day, and whose fate, pathetic at all times, out-tragedies almost any other in the history of letters. She was seized with hydrophobia from the bite of her dog, on a railroad train; and made a long journey home in the paroxysms of that agonizing disease, which ended in her death after she reached New York. But this was after her reign had ended, and no such black shadow was cast forward upon Pfaff's, whose name often figured in the verse and the epigrammatically paragraphed prose of the 'Saturday Press'. I felt that as a contributor and at least a brevet Bohemian I ought not to go home without visiting the famous place, and witnessing if I could not share the revels of my comrades. As I neither drank beer nor smoked, my part in the carousal was limited to a German pancake, which I found they had very good at Pfaff's, and to listening to the whirling words of my commensals, at the long board spread for the Bohemians in a cavernous space under the pavement. There were writers for the 'Saturday Press' and for Vanity Fair (a hopefully comic paper of that day), and some of the artists who drew for the illustrated periodicals. Nothing of their talk remains with me, but the impression remains that it was not so good talk as I had heard in Boston. At one moment of the orgy, which went but slowly for an orgy, we were joined by some belated Bohemians whom the others made a great clamor over; I was given to understand they were just recovered from a fearful debauch; their locks were still damp from the wet towels used to restore them, and their eyes were very frenzied. I was presented to these types, who neither said nor did anything worthy of their awful appearance, but dropped into seats at the table, and ate of the supper with an appetite that seemed poor. I stayed hoping vainly for worse things till eleven o'clock, and then I rose and took my leave of a literary condition that had distinctly disappointed me. I do not say that it may not have been wickeder and wittier than I found it; I only report what I saw and heard in Bohemia on my first visit to New York, and I know that my acquaintance with it was not exhaustive. When I came the next year the Saturday Press was no more, and the editor and his contributors had no longer a common centre. The best of the young fellows whom I met there confessed, in a pleasant exchange of letters which we had afterwards, that he thought the pose a vain and unprofitable one; and when the Press was revived, after the war, it was without any of the old Bohemian characteristics except that of not paying for material. It could not last long upon these terms, and again it passed away, and still waits its second palingenesis.

The editor passed away too, not long after, and the thing that he had inspired altogether ceased to be. He was a man of a certain sardonic power, and used it rather fiercely and freely, with a joy probably more apparent than real in the pain it gave. In my last knowledge of him he was much milder than when I first knew him, and I have the feeling that he too came to own before he died that man cannot live by snapping-turtle alone. He was kind to some neglected talents, and befriended them with a vigor and a zeal which he would have been the last to let you call generous. The chief of these was Walt Whitman, who, when the Saturday Press took it up, had as hopeless a cause with the critics on either side of the ocean as any man could have. It was not till long afterwards that his English admirers began to discover him, and to make his countrymen some noisy reproaches for ignoring him; they were wholly in the dark concerning him when the Saturday Press, which first stood his friend, and the young men whom the Press gathered about it, made him their cult. No doubt he was more valued because he was so offensive in some ways than he would have been if he had been in no way offensive, but it remains a fact that they celebrated him quite as much as was good for them. He was often at Pfaff's with them, and the night of my visit he was the chief fact of my experience. I did not know he was there till I was on my way out, for he did not sit at the table under the pavement, but at the head of one farther into the room. There, as I passed, some friendly fellow stopped me and named me to him, and I remember how he leaned back in his chair, and reached out his great hand to me, as if he were going to give it me for good and all. He had a fine head, with a cloud of Jovian hair upon it, and a branching beard and mustache, and gentle eyes that looked most kindly into mine, and seemed to wish the liking which I instantly gave him, though we hardly passed a word, and our acquaintance was summed up in that glance and the grasp of his mighty fist upon my hand. I doubt if he had any notion who or what I was beyond the fact that I was a young poet of some sort, but he may possibly have remembered seeing my name printed after some very Heinesque verses in the Press. I did not meet him again for twenty years, and then I had only a moment with him when he was reading the proofs of his poems in Boston. Some years later I saw him for the last time, one day after his lecture on Lincoln, in that city, when he came down from the platform to speak with some handshaking friends who gathered about him. Then and always he gave me the sense of a sweet and true soul, and I felt in him a spiritual dignity which I will not try to reconcile with his printing in the forefront of his book a passage from a private letter of Emerson's, though I believe he would not have seen such a thing as most other men would, or thought ill of it in another. The spiritual purity which I felt in him no less than the dignity is something that I will no more try to reconcile with what denies it in his page; but such things we may well leave to the adjustment of finer balances than we have at hand. I will make sure only of the greatest benignity in the presence of the man. The apostle of the rough, the uncouth, was the gentlest person; his barbaric yawp, translated into the terms of social encounter, was an address of singular quiet, delivered in a voice of winning and endearing friendliness.

As to his work itself, I suppose that I do not think it so valuable in effect as in intention. He was a liberating force, a very "imperial anarch" in literature; but liberty is never anything but a means, and what Whitman achieved was a means and not an end, in what must be called his verse. I like his prose, if there is a difference, much better; there he is of a genial and comforting quality, very rich and cordial, such as I felt him to be when I met him in person. His verse seems to me not poetry, but the materials of poetry, like one's emotions; yet I would not misprize it, and I am glad to own that I have had moments of great pleasure in it. Some French critic quoted in the Saturday Press (I cannot think of his name) said the best thing of him when he said that he made you a partner of the enterprise, for that is precisely what he does, and that is what alienates and what endears in him, as you like or dislike the partnership. It is still something neighborly, brotherly, fatherly, and so I felt him to be when the benign old man looked on me and spoke to me.

III.

That night at Pfaff's must have been the last of the Bohemians for me, and it was the last of New York authorship too, for the time. I do not know why I should not have imagined trying to see Curtis, whom I knew so much by heart, and whom I adored, but I may not have had the courage, or I may have heard that he was out of town; Bryant, I believe, was then out of the country; but at any rate I did not attempt him either. The Bohemians were the beginning and the end of the story for me, and to tell the truth I did not like the story. I remember that as I sat at that table under the pavement, in Pfaff's beer-cellar, and listened to the wit that did not seem very funny, I thought of the dinner with Lowell, the breakfast with Fields, the supper at the Autocrat's, and felt that I had fallen very far. In fact it can do no harm at this distance of time to confess that it seemed to me then, and for a good while afterwards, that a person who had seen the men and had the things said before him that I had in Boston, could not keep himself too carefully in cotton; and this was what I did all the following winter, though of course it was a secret between me and me. I dare say it was not the worst thing I could have done, in some respects.

My sojourn in New York could not have been very long, and the rest of it was mainly given to viewing the monuments of the city from the windows of omnibuses and the platforms of horse-cars. The world was so simple then that there were perhaps only a half dozen cities that had horse-cars in them, and I travelled in those conveyances at New York with an unfaded zest, even after my journeys back and forth between Boston and Cambridge. I have not the least notion where I went or what I saw, but I suppose that it was up and down the ugly east and west avenues, then lying open to the eye in all the hideousness now partly concealed by the elevated roads, and that I found them very stately and handsome. Indeed, New York was really handsomer then than it is now, when it has so many more pieces of beautiful architecture, for at that day the sky-scrapers were not yet, and there was a fine regularity in the streets that these brute bulks have robbed of all shapeliness. Dirt and squalor there were a plenty, but there was infinitely more comfort. The long succession of cross streets was yet mostly secure from business, after you passed Clinton Place; commerce was just beginning to show itself in Union Square, and Madison Square was still the home of the McFlimsies, whose kin and kind dwelt unmolested in the brownstone stretches of Fifth Avenue. I tried hard to imagine them from the acquaintance Mr. Butler's poem had given me, and from the knowledge the gentle satire of The 'Potiphar Papers' had spread broadcast through a community shocked by the excesses of our best society; it was not half so bad then as the best now, probably. But I do not think I made very much of it, perhaps because most of the people who ought to have been in those fine mansions were away at the seaside and the mountains.

The mountains I had seen on my way down from Canada, but the sea-side not, and it would never do to go home without visiting some famous summer resort. I must have fixed upon Long Branch because I must have heard of it as then the most fashionable; and one afternoon I took the boat for that place. By this means I not only saw sea-bathing for the first time, but I saw a storm at sea: a squall struck us so suddenly that it blew away all the camp-stools of the forward promenade; it was very exciting, and I long meant to use in literature the black wall of cloud that settled on the water before us like a sort of portable midnight; I now throw it away upon the reader, as it were; it never would come in anywhere. I stayed all night at Long Branch, and I had a bath the next morning before breakfast: an extremely cold one, with a life-line to keep me against the undertow. In this rite I had the company of a young New-Yorker, whom I had met on the boat coming down, and who was of the light, hopeful, adventurous business type which seems peculiar to the city, and which has always attracted me. He told me much about his life, and how he lived, and what it cost him to live. He had a large room at a fashionable boardinghouse, and he paid fourteen dollars a week. In Columbus I had such a room at such a house, and paid three and a half, and I thought it a good deal. But those were the days before the war, when America was the cheapest country in the world, and the West was incredibly inexpensive.

After a day of lonely splendor at this scene of fashion and gaiety, I went back to New York, and took the boat for Albany on my way home. I noted that I had no longer the vivid interest in nature and human nature which I had felt in setting out upon my travels, and I said to myself that this was from having a mind so crowded with experiences and impressions that it could receive no more; and I really suppose that if the happiest phrase had offered itself to me at some moments, I should scarcely have looked about me for a land-scape or a figure to fit it to. I was very glad to get back to my dear little city in the West (I found it seething in an August sun that was hot enough to have calcined the limestone State House), and to all the friends I was so fond of.

IV.

I did what I could to prove myself unworthy of them by refusing their invitations, and giving myself wholly to literature, during the early part of the winter that followed; and I did not realize my error till the invitations ceased to come, and I found myself in an unbroken intellectual solitude. The worst of it was that an ungrateful Muse did little in return for the sacrifices I made her, and the things I now wrote were not liked by the editors I sent them to. The editorial taste is not always the test of merit, but it is the only one we have, and I am not saying the editors were wrong in my case. There were then such a very few places where you could market your work: the Atlantic in Boston and Harper's in New York were the magazines that paid, though the Independent newspaper bought literary material; the Saturday Press printed it without buying, and so did the old Knickerbocker Magazine, though there was pecuniary good-will in both these cases. I toiled much that winter over a story I had long been writing, and at last sent it to the Atlantic, which had published five poems for me the year before. After some weeks, or it may have been months, I got it back with a note saying that the editors had the less regret in returning it because they saw that in the May number of the Knickerbocker the first chapter of the story had appeared. Then I remembered that, years before, I had sent this chapter to that magazine, as a sketch to be printed by itself, and afterwards had continued the story from it. I had never heard of its acceptance, and supposed of course that it was rejected; but on my second visit to New York I called at the Knickerbocker office, and a new editor, of those that the magazine was always having in the days of its failing fortunes, told me that he had found my sketch in rummaging about in a barrel of his predecessors manuscripts, and had liked it, and printed it. He said that there were fifteen dollars coming to me for that sketch, and might he send the money to me? I said that he might, though I do not see, to this day, why he did not give it me on the spot; and he made a very small minute in a very large sheet of paper (really like Dick Swiveller), and promised I should have it that night; but I sailed the next day for Liverpool without it. I sailed without the money for some verses that Vanity Fair bought of me, but I hardly expected that, for the editor, who was then Artemus Ward, had frankly told me in taking my address that ducats were few at that moment with Vanity Fair. I was then on my way to be consul at Venice, where I spent the next four years in a vigilance for Confederate privateers which none of them ever surprised. I had asked for the consulate at Munich, where I hoped to steep myself yet longer in German poetry, but when my appointment came, I found it was for Rome. I was very glad to get Rome even; but the income of the office was in fees, and I thought I had better go on to Washington and find out how much the fees amounted to. People in Columbus who had been abroad said that on five hundred dollars you could live in Rome like a prince, but I doubted this; and when I learned at the State Department that the fees of the Roman consulate came to only three hundred, I perceived that I could not live better than a baron, probably, and I despaired. The kindly chief of the consular bureau said that the President's secretaries, Mr. John Nicolay and Mr. John Hay, were interested in my appointment, and he advised my going over to the White House and seeing them. I lost no time in doing that, and I learned that as young Western men they were interested in me because I was a young Western man who had done something in literature, and they were willing to help me for that reason, and for no other that I ever knew. They proposed my going to Venice; the salary was then seven hundred and fifty, but they thought they could get it put up to a thousand. In the end they got it put up to fifteen hundred, and so I went to Venice, where if I did not live like a prince on that income, I lived a good deal more like a prince than I could have done at Rome on a fifth of it.

If the appointment was not present fortune, it was the beginning of the best luck I have had in the world, and I am glad to owe it all to those friends of my verse, who could have been no otherwise friends of me. They were then beginning very early careers of distinction which have not been wholly divided. Mr. Nicolay could have been about twenty-five, and Mr. Hay nineteen or twenty. No one dreamed as yet of the opportunity opening to them in being so constantly near the man whose life they have written, and with whose fame they have imperishably interwrought their names. I remember the sobered dignity of the one, and the humorous gaiety of the other, and how we had some young men's joking and laughing together, in the anteroom where they received me, with the great soul entering upon its travail beyond the closed door. They asked me if I had ever seen the President, and I said that I had seen him at Columbus, the year before; but I could not say how much I should like to see him again, and thank him for the favor which I had no claim to at his hands, except such as the slight campaign biography I had written could be thought to have given me. That day or another, as I left my friends, I met him in the corridor without, and he looked at the space I was part of with his ineffably melancholy eyes, without knowing that I was the indistinguishable person in whose "integrity and abilities he had reposed such special confidence" as to have appointed him consul for Venice and the ports of the Lombardo-Venetian Kingdom, though he might have recognized the terms of my commission if I had reminded him of them. I faltered a moment in my longing to address him, and then I decided that every one who forebore to speak needlessly to him, or to shake his hand, did him a kindness; and I wish I could be as sure of the wisdom of all my past behavior as I am of that piece of it. He walked up to the water-cooler that stood in the corner, and drew himself a full goblet from it, which he poured down his throat with a backward tilt of his head, and then went wearily within doors. The whole affair, so simple, has always remained one of a certain pathos in my memory, and I would rather have seen Lincoln in that unconscious moment than on some statelier occasion.

V.

I went home to Ohio; and sent on the bond I was to file in the Treasury Department; but it was mislaid there, and to prevent another chance of that kind I carried on the duplicate myself. It was on my second visit that I met the generous young Irishman William D. O'Connor, at the house of my friend Piatt, and heard his ardent talk. He was one of the promising men of that day, and he had written an anti-slavery novel in the heroic mood of Victor Hugo, which greatly took my fancy; and I believe he wrote poems too. He had not yet risen to be the chief of Walt Whitman's champions outside of the Saturday Press, but he had already espoused the theory of Bacon's authorship of Shakespeare, then newly exploited by the poor lady of Bacon's name, who died constant to it in an insane asylum. He used to speak of the reputed dramatist as "the fat peasant of Stratford," and he was otherwise picturesque of speech in a measure that consoled, if it did not convince. The great war was then full upon us, and when in the silences of our literary talk its awful breath was heard, and its shadow fell upon the hearth where we gathered round the first fires of autumn, O'Connor would lift his beautiful head with a fine effect of prophecy, and say, "Friends, I feel a sense of victory in the air." He was not wrong; only the victory was for the other aide.

Who beside O'Connor shared in these saddened symposiums I cannot tell now; but probably other young journalists and office-holders, intending litterateurs, since more or less extinct. I make certain only of the young Boston publisher who issued a very handsome edition of 'Leaves of Grass', and then failed promptly if not consequently. But I had already met, in my first sojourn at the capital, a young journalist who had given hostages to poetry, and whom I was very glad to see and proud to know. Mr. Stedman and I were talking over that meeting the other day, and I can be surer than I might have been without his memory, that I found him at a friend's house, where he was nursing himself for some slight sickness, and that I sat by his bed while our souls launched together into the joyful realms of hope and praise. In him I found the quality of Boston, the honor and passion of literature, and not a mere pose of the literary life; and the world knows without my telling how true he has been to his ideal of it. His earthly mission then was to write letters from Washington for the New York World, which started in life as a good young evening paper, with a decided religious tone, so that the Saturday Press could call it the Night-blooming Serious. I think Mr. Stedman wrote for its editorial page at times, and his relation to it as a Washington correspondent had an authority which is wanting to the function in these days of perfected telegraphing. He had not yet achieved that seat in the Stock Exchange whose possession has justified his recourse to business, and has helped him to mean something more single in literature than many more singly devoted to it. I used sometimes to speak about that with another eager young author in certain middle years when we were chafing in editorial harness, and we always decided that Stedman had the best of it in being able to earn his living in a sort so alien to literature that he could come to it unjaded, and with a gust unspoiled by kindred savors. But no man shapes his own life, and I dare say that Stedman may have been all the time envying us our tripods from his high place in the Stock Exchange. What is certain is that he has come to stand for literature and to embody New York in it as no one else does. In a community which seems never to have had a conscious relation to letters, he has kept the faith with dignity and fought the fight with constant courage. Scholar and poet at once, he has spoken to his generation with authority which we can forget only in the charm which makes us forget everything else.

But his fame was still before him when we met, and I could bring to him an admiration for work which had not yet made itself known to so many; but any admirer was welcome. We talked of what we had done, and each said how much he liked certain thing of the other's; I even seized my advantage of his helplessness to read him a poem of mine which I had in my pocket; he advised me where to place it; and if the reader will not think it an unfair digression, I will tell here what became of that poem, for I think its varied fortunes were amusing, and I hope my own sufferings and final triumph with it will not be without encouragement to the young literary endeavorer. It was a poem called, with no prophetic sense of fitness,

"Forlorn," and I tried it first with the 'Atlantic Monthly', which would not have it. Then I offered it in person to a former editor of 'Harper's Monthly', but he could not see his advantage in it, and I carried it overseas to Venice with me. From that point I sent it to all the English magazines as steadily as the post could carry it away and bring it back. On my way home, four years later, I took it to London with me, where a friend who knew Lewes, then just beginning with the 'Fortnightly Review', sent it to him for me. It was promptly returned, with a letter wholly reserved as to its quality, but full of a poetic gratitude for my wish to contribute to the Fortnightly. Then I heard that a certain Mr. Lucas was about to start a magazine, and I offered the poem to him. The kindest letter of acceptance followed me to America, and I counted upon fame and fortune as usual, when the news of Mr. Lucas's death came. I will not poorly joke an effect from my poem in the fact; but the fact remains. By this time I was a writer in the office of the 'Nation' newspaper, and after I left this place to be Mr. Fields's assistant on the Atlantic, I sent my poem to the Nation, where it was printed at last. In such scant measure as my verses have pleased it has found rather unusual favor, and I need not say that its misfortunes endeared it to its author.

But all this is rather far away from my first meeting with Stedman in Washington. Of course I liked him, and I thought him very handsome and fine, with a full beard cut in the fashion he has always worn it, and with poet's eyes lighting an aquiline profile. Afterwards, when I saw him afoot, I found him of a worldly splendor in dress, and envied him, as much as I could envy him anything, the New York tailor whose art had clothed him: I had a New York tailor too, but with a difference. He had a worldly dash along with his supermundane gifts, which took me almost as much, and all the more because I could see that he valued himself nothing upon it. He was all for literature, and for literary men as the superiors of every one. I must have opened my heart to him a good deal, for when I told him how the newspaper I had written for from Canada and New England had ceased to print my letters, he said, "Think of a man like sitting in judgment on a man like you!" I thought of it, and was avenged if not comforted; and at any rate I liked Stedman's standing up so stiffly for the honor of a craft that is rather too limp in some of its votaries.

I suppose it was he who introduced me to the Stoddards, whom I met in New York just before I sailed, and who were then in the glow of their early fame as poets. They knew about my poor beginnings, and they were very, very good to me. Stoddard went with me to Franklin Square, and gave the sanction of his presence to the ineffectual offer of my poem there. But what I relished most was the long talks I had with them both about authorship in all its phases, and the exchange of delight in this poem and that, this novel and that, with gay, wilful runs away to make some wholly irrelevant joke, or fire puns into the air at no mark whatever. Stoddard had then a fame, with the sweetness of personal affection in it, from the lyrics and the odes that will perhaps best keep him known, and Mrs. Stoddard was beginning to make her distinct and special quality felt in the magazines, in verse and fiction. In both it seems to me that she has failed of the recognition which her work merits. Her tales and novels have in them a foretaste of realism, which was too strange for the palate of their day, and is now too familiar, perhaps. It is a peculiar fate, and would form the scheme of a pretty study in the history of literature. But in whatever she did she left the stamp of a talent like no other, and of a personality disdainful of literary environment. In a time when most of us had to write like Tennyson, or Longfellow, or Browning, she never would write like any one but herself.

I remember very well the lodging over a corner of Fourth Avenue and some downtown street where I visited these winning and gifted people, and tasted the pleasure of their racy talk, and the hospitality of their good-will toward all literature, which certainly did not leave me out. We sat before their grate in the chill of the last October days, and they set each other on to one wild flight of wit after another, and again I bathed my delighted spirit in the atmosphere of a realm where for the time at least no

> "— — rumor of oppression or defeat, Of
> unsuccessful or successful war,"

could penetrate. I liked the Stoddards because they were frankly not of that Bohemia which I disliked so much, and thought it of no promise or validity; and because I was fond of their poetry and found them in it. I liked the absolutely literary keeping of their lives. He had then, and for long after, a place in the Custom house, but he was no more of that than Lamb was of India House. He belonged to that better world where there is no interest but letters, and which was as much like heaven for me as anything I could think of.

The meetings with the Stoddards repeated themselves when I came back to sail from New York, early in November. Mixed up with the cordial pleasure of them in my memory is a sense of the cold and wet outdoors, and the misery of being in those infamous New York streets, then as for long afterwards the squalidest in the world. The last night I saw my friends they told me of the tragedy which had just happened at the camp in the City Hall Park. Fitz James O'Brien, the brilliant young Irishman who had dazzled us with his story of "The Diamond Lens," and frozen our blood with his ingenious tale of a ghost—"What was It"—a ghost that could be felt and heard, but not seen—had enlisted for the war, and risen to be an officer with the swift process of the first days of it. In that camp he had just then shot and killed a man for some infraction of discipline, and it was uncertain what the end would be. He was acquitted, however, and it is known how he afterwards died of lockjaw from a wound received in battle.

VI.

Before this last visit in New York there was a second visit to Boston, which I need not dwell upon, because it was chiefly a revival of the impressions of the first. Again I saw the Fieldses in their home; again the Autocrat in his, and Lowell now beneath his own roof, beside the study fire where I was so often to sit with him in coming years. At dinner (which we had at two o'clock) the talk turned upon my appointment, and he said of me to his wife: "Think of his having got Stillman's place! We ought to put poison in his wine," and he told me of the wish the painter had to go to Venice and follow up Ruskin's work there in a book of his own. But he would not let me feel very guilty, and I will not pretend that I had any personal regret for my good fortune.

The place was given me perhaps because I had not nearly so many other gifts as he who lost it, and who was at once artist, critic, journalist, traveller, and eminently each. I met him afterwards in Rome, which the powers bestowed upon him instead of Venice, and he forgave me, though I do not know whether he forgave the powers. We walked far and long over the Campagna, and I felt the charm of a most uncommon mind in talk which came out richest and fullest in the presence of the wild nature which he loved and knew so much better than most other men. I think that the book he would have written about Venice is forever to be regretted, and I do not at all console myself for its loss with the book I have written myself.

At Lowell's table that day they spoke of what sort of winter I should find in Venice, and he inclined to the belief that I should want a fire there. On his study hearth a very brisk one burned when we went back to it, and kept out the chill of a cold easterly storm. We looked through one of the windows at the rain, and he said he could remember standing and looking out of that window at such a storm when he was a child; for he was born in that house, and his life had kept coming back to it. He died in it, at last.

In a lifting of the rain he walked with me down to the village, as he always called the denser part of the town about Harvard Square, and saw me aboard a horse-car for Boston. Before we parted he gave me two charges: to open my mouth when I began to speak Italian, and to think well of women. He said that our race spoke its own tongue with its teeth shut, and so failed to master the languages that wanted freer utterance. As to women, he said there were unworthy ones, but a good woman was the best thing in the world, and a man was always the better for honoring women.